Ellen's Story

i

Chronicler Publishing

For information address:
Chronicler Publishing
Jones Beach,
RR 1 Evansburg,
Alberta, Canada, T0E 0T0
www.chroniclerpublishing.com

ISBN: 9780980953435

Dedication
to
Dolly for her information and friendship

ELLEN'S STORY
Dianne Osborne

Author's Note: This story is strictly fictitious. However, there are incidents based on fact. Andrew's accident and the black butter are excerpts from my family's histories. The crypt and fuel depot are excerpts from my husband's sojourn in the Canadian army during World War II. I've had to do some ad-libbing to suit the story's fictitious circumstances.

I also realize that some of the war incidents could not have been told during the war as I have done in this story. It would have been too detrimental to the allies. But this is fiction–ah, sweet fiction.

Ellen's Story

CHAPTER 1

The shed door slammed shut with a bang. We really didn't hear it but then again we didn't hear all the rest of the sounds that rattled around in our sub-conscience—a state of mind we all were in for days, months and what seemed like years.

In one of my childhood picture storybooks there was an illustration of Mr. Wind with his cheeks puffed out to the fullest in order to bend the trees and whip up the dirt. In my mind's eye I pictured Mr. Wind blowing the shed door shut then scurrying around the grassless yard to throw dirt at our windows—at times giving us cause for concern—then sneak around the side of the shed to blow the door shut again. In his whirling and twirling the tall lifeless grass of the endless prairie would bow down to him almost lying prostrate. The young saplings Pa had planted for a windbreak would also pay homage to Mr. Wind as he hurriedly passed them by on his way back to the shed to blow the door shut again. As if trying to apologize for the havoc he was causing he would sing us a song in the eaves of the house.

You really couldn't hate the wind. When he was in a gentle mood he would flip the newly washed sheets Ma had hung on a wire line not far from the house. The crack of the whipped sheets was like a rifle shot and if I had been Ma and Pa's only boy instead of their only girl, I might have imagined the cracking sheets as the enemy, run for cover then shoot back with my own wooden pistol.

During the course of Mr. Wind's gentler moods he couldn't resist a little bit of mischief by giving an extra twist to the sheets releasing them from the clutches of the clothespins. This would send them flying and Ma would find them wrapped around a fence post, draped over the plough or caught in the bare and prickly arms of the pathetic looking bush that was supposed to be our raspberries. I would be sent to look for clothespin parts that the sheets had attempted to take with them.

Ma would retrieve the wayward sheets to replace them on our beds and after having had a good wash in a small basin half full of water, it was a joy to crawl in between sheets smelling of fresh air and sunshine. You couldn't help but have a soft spot for Mr. Wind. But other days, like this day, he would team up with Mistress Sun to blow her hot air around mixing it with the dirt. Because of the flying dust, the doors and windows had to be kept shut which when the wind was showing his gentler side were kept open to catch a breeze soothing your hot, flushed face.

I sat on my stool by the living room window watching the dust. On calmer days I could see the neighbors. But not today. It wasn't as bad as some days but bad enough to make me feel as if Ma and Pa and I were the only living souls left.

Pa stirred on the old couch where he had been sleeping most of the afternoon. He struggled to sit up, then sat for a moment, blinking his eyes and trying to capture the reason for moving in the first place.

Slowly he raised himself on his thin legs to carefully take his skeleton-like frame out through the kitchen. I heard the outside door slam and knew Pa was on his way to the backhouse. There was no other reason to go outside.

A few minutes later Pa stumbled into the kitchen and fell onto a chair by the table breathing deeply, trying to catch his breath. Once his breathing became easier he would fold his arms on the table to rest his head on them. There he would sit for up to an hour. I think he must doze off to a light sleep as he sat so still.

I continued my viewless watch for a few minutes longer then returned to looking at the open book on my lap. It was called "The Birds of Western Canada." Although there were very few birds around now that the hot, dry weather had ruined many of their habitat, it was a joy to look at the bright pictures of Canada Geese resting on a prairie slough before continuing on their journey to their north summer home. Then there would be the red-winged blackbird on the bulrushes along a ditch; the sparrow feeding her young in a nest sheltered in a lush cottonwood tree. The green of the grass, the silver of the waters and blue of the sky dotted with white fully 'cotton ball' clouds made me feel better. Made me remember how it was and gave me hope that maybe someday it would be again.

As my eyes left the window on the way to my book, they caught the sight of the sofa Pa had been lying on. A small chicken feather lay at the edge of the cushion where it had escaped from its casing, one of the many that had left to make a shallow hollow where Pa's head had laid.

The upholstery on the cushions was becoming loose and wrinkled due to the pressure of Pa's shoulders, hips and heels on the stuffing. During the last year or so the sofa had been Pa's refuge.

Ma rarely came into the living room. She puttered and tinkered a great deal in the kitchen. She loved to cook but now with money so scarce and no gardens to speak of, she sat most of the time in her wooden rocking chair facing the big old black cooking range, no doubt thinking back when she was able to bring a brown crisp turkey, loaves of crusty bread and delicate cream puffs out of its oven to feed us and the neighbours on a Sunday afternoon.

The clock on the buffet cupboard that had to stand in the living room, since we didn't have a dining room, struck five o'clock. Ma heaved herself out of her rocking chair mumbling something about getting supper ready.

It was a long time before I understood why Ma was so overweight. She didn't eat any more than Pa and I did. There wasn't any extra food in the house. Each day we sat down and gave thanks for our rations of beans and biscuits. But Ma continued to be a hefty woman.

Ma didn't like to start the range on such a windy day as sparks coming from the chimney could start a prairie fire, the homesteaders'' worst fear. So we ate our beans cold on cold biscuits and each washed it down with a small glass of cold milk that was stored in the well. There was little water in the well but enough to keep a small pail of milk from souring.

The evening was as hot as the day and would continue quite warm until the wee small hours of the next day. The refreshing coolness of the night did not last long after the sun began to rise in a blaze of fire. The horizon would be red turning to gold as the sun made its way across the blue bowl of sky that covered this land of everlasting wind and dry grass.

The closeness of the heat and wind seemed to drain the energy from our bodies and so our evening was spent much the same as the day. Pa returned to the sofa, Ma to her rocking chair and I half-heartedly returned to my book. But I was more in the mood for daydreaming. I tried to think back to how it was before the wind. It was hard to do with the wind still blowing outside so I thought of one of the first times we encountered the Black Blizzard.

The first one that came set the pattern for all the rest. The morning was full of sunshine with a gentle breeze. Pa had finished planting his crop of wheat not too many days earlier. Ma's garden had twigs marking the rows where vegetables and a few flowers had been planted. Pa felt that since he was able to work the stubble in last fall he should have a better crop this year. Rain had been scarce last year but enough to make kernels. However the quality and quantity was not there. A fair amount of snow came during the winter but the hot dry spring had soon made short work of what moisture there had been.

Ellen's Story

Ma had been able to buy some special flower seeds that she said would attract the bees better than any other kind of flower she knew of. How the bees would know the flowers were here was more than I could figure out.

Sometime during that afternoon, Pa came into the house with a worried look on his face.

"I don't like it, Katie," he said. "There is not a breath of wind outside. It's so still it's almost suffocating."

They both went to the kitchen window that faced the south. Nothing could be seen but out of the corner of his eye Pa saw something black to the west. In a couple of strides he was out the screen door. Seconds later he was back in hollering:

"Close the windows and doors and gather in the kitchen. I don't like the looks of the horizon." With that he took the stairs two and three at a time to close the windows that let light and air into our bedroom.

Ma attended to the living room then came to close the kitchen window.

I was eight years old, too small to be of any help except to stay out of the way. I stood close to the small wooden kitchen table in wonder. And then the fear began.

Pa had just started down the stairs and Ma was still struggling with the kitchen window when the deafening roar was upon us bringing with it complete darkness—darkness that enveloped you in its noisy arms. My ears hurt, my eyes hurt. I couldn't tell if they were open or shut. I was being hemmed in; I couldn't cry, I couldn't breathe. Pressure on my chest prohibited it. Then there was a soft pressure and I knew somehow Ma had found me. Soon Pa was with us too. It was better but it was a frightful feeling to be in the middle of something you didn't understand.

5

Dianne Osborne

I knew my eyes had been open when I began to see a lightening of the darkness. With the light came the quiet and the gentle breeze of the morning was with us once more. It was like waking from a bad dream; did it really happen?

Pa let out a slow whistle as if he had been holding his breath. "Wow! That was something else again, eh, Katie, me love? Hey there, Sprig. (Pa always called me Sprig because I was as skinny as he was). "I think you'd better get your face washed before I begin to think I have a little black girl for a daughter."

Ma went to the water pail to dip out some water for the basin. She let out a cry. "Oh, it's full of mud."

"By jiggins, so it is," said Pa, as he came to look.

Picking up the pail he headed for the door and the well. Passing the small white wood framed mirror near the door, Pa caught a glimpse of himself and let out his own roar, a roar so much more pleasant than the one we had just experienced. "Well, girls, I guess I had better take my own advice about washing faces." Chuckling he went out to get some water.

Once the dirt was removed from our eyes and mouths and noses we surveyed the house to find that a broom and dust rag were to be our companions for the rest of the day.

We fell exhausted that night into beds that had to be stripped, shook vigorously, and then remade. There had been no time to wash the bedding. That would have to be part of tomorrow's chores. So we slept with the smell of dust close at hand.

Pa had to reseed his fifty acres again. He would hitch the horses to the stone boat that held the few left over bags of seed than lead them to the field. Here he took his hand seeder, fitted it to his shoulders, filled it with grain and walked the length of the field back and forth till it was done. This time it was sowed a little thinner. Pa was

6

always optimistic; with some rain he would have as good a crop as last year.

We did get some rain; enough to germinate the seed to send forth thin green arms searching for sunshine and moisture. However, the hot sun and wind soon matured the plants. There wasn't much straw but there were some kernels. I think Pa got his seed back.

We had another blizzard in the fall. This time we were more prepared. After becoming aware of the stillness of the air we spotted the huge black cloud on the horizon rolling along like black-brown balls of fire. Storm clouds are blue-black in color. Although they look menacing and eerie they quietly glide into your presence to give you a chilly feeling. The dust clouds rolled with a frightening roar like that of a thousand lions and you felt hot and sticky all over.

We rushed for the house to close windows and doors and met in the kitchen huddling together, my face in Ma's apron, smelling her warm body and although it may not have been as sweet an aroma as it should have been, it was still Ma and I was not so frightened.

Winter came with lots and lots of snow. Farmers' hopes were once again raised. With all this moisture crops should be good this year. But when spring came, the hot sun came too. We were hit with another dust blizzard.

This time I was at school. We all were able to recognize the signs so it took no coaxing from the teacher to close the doors and windows of our one room schoolhouse. We all took our seats again remaining there with our heads resting on our folded arms, which in turn rested on the desks. I put my pinafore apron over my head, as did some of the other girls.

Although I was a year older and knew what to expect, it was still a terrifying experience. I think we all were frightened even the teacher but she had to put on a brave front. After the storm had passed she cheerfully said, "Well, that wasn't so bad. Now let's get the broom and dust rags and clean up a bit before we finish our lessons."

The Black Blizzards, as the dust storms were called because they were much like a snowstorm except there was dust and dirt in the air instead of snow, all seemed pretty much to be the same. The stillness that gave you a warning was followed by darkness and noise that in turn was followed by cleaning house and the return of a pleasant day weatherize.

One particular dust storm had a funny end to it but it was also the most tragic one for us.

Pa was out in the field south of the house harrowing his thinly seeded crop. Like all the neighbours, Pa thought that a little bit of seed was better than no seed. Who knows? If the rains came these few seeds could yield enough for a better planting next year. So Pa was out hurrying to cover the seeds before the birds and wind took them away.

Ma decided to wash clothes and make butter. We still had one cow. She didn't give much milk but enough that we could make butter once in a while by saving a little cream each day and storing it in the well to keep cold. Butter was becoming a treat so we made small batches before the cream soured.

Our washing machine was a half-moon shape, its rounded bottom braced on A-frame legs. A tight fitting lid on the flat side covered the clothes and water. On the side a long handle was provided so that the 'lady' of the house could swing it right and left putting the tub into a swaying motion. This she would do for ten to fifteen minutes enabling the clothes to swish around in the water and hopefully get clean.

On this long handle Pa had fixed a clamp to hold a quart sealer. Ma put the cream into the sealer, clamped it to the handle and made butter and washed clothes at the same time. While she wrung the clothes out with her strong capable hands she would unclamp the sealer, give it to me and I would continue to shake it manually until she had hung the clothes out on the line and put in another bundle of clothes in the machine. Then back to the handle went the sealer until butter formed.

The butter had clotted so she left the washing machine stand idle while she washed and salted the butter. This particular day she put the butter into the mold with a flower on top. Having packed it in good she then flipped it onto a plate. It was now ready for lunch.

At this moment we both noticed the stillness in the air. Ma looked out the window and saw Pa running with the horses towards the barn.

"Come, Ellen," she said. "We'll run to the barn and help Pa unharness the horses so he can get to the house faster." She reached for my hand and headed for the door as she was explaining all this and we ran for the barn too.

We just barely finished unharnessing when the storm hit. Pa gathered us together in his arms in the nearest stall to where we had been standing. It had been used at one time by two of our many cows we had had at one time. There was no familiar smell of a warm body or warm milk. The wind had taken that all away. But if there hadn't been so much dust in the air we would have been able to smell the horses that were in the next stall. All we could smell was the sweat from each other. How is it that you can smell these smells long after your loved one—human or animal—has gone? And how wonderful to smell them again, even if it is just in your mind. It seems to bring them back for just a moment.

After everything settled we headed for the house. That was when Ma remembered that the windows and doors didn't get shut. Then she remembered the butter.. She began to run, afraid of what she was going to find yet wanting to know in a hurry.

9

There on its plate with a pretty flower embedded on top was the butter—not golden yellow but black as a lump of coal.

"I'll just scrape the outside carefully so that we'll be able to use the inside."

Ma sat down and cried when she discovered that the butter was full of the dirt and black all the way through.

Pa saw the funny side of it and roared with laughter. I sympathized with Ma. We had worked hard for that pound of butter and it would be at least a week before we would have enough cream to make more. I didn't see anything funny about it.

"Hey, Sprig. Don't look so glum. Our one lone pig out there needs a little fattening up so he gets the butter for his supper." And out Pa went to feed the pig.

In a few moments he was back. One look at his face and even I knew something was terribly wrong.

He sat the dirty butter plate on the table then sat down on a chair beside the table. He leaned his head on his arms and sat there. Just sat there. He made neither noise nor any movement.

Alarmed, Ma hesitatingly touched his arm. "Kelly, whatever is the matter? You've never acted this way before." Pa slowly raised his head and looked right into her face, a look of agony in his own and said "Catherine" (Yes, something was definitely wrong. He used her full name.) "Catherine" he said again, "the seed is gone from the fields. I don't have any more seed. I don't have money to buy seed. There is no seed in the country to buy and what there is, is very expensive. I cannot borrow seed from the neighbours; I'm in debt up to my ears to them already. I can't ask for any more favors that I know I won't be able to return for years. Catherine, we are finished." And he returned his head to his arms.

Ellen's Story

Ma sat a long time staring at him with her mouth open and eyes wide. I just sat and looked at them. I was eleven years old. I didn't understand everything but I knew it was bad.

I never heard Pa laugh again.

CHAPTER 2

The soft closing of the buffet drawer woke me from my reverie. Ma had put away her Bible and journal in the drawer that also held a few tablecloths and doilies, niceties that were rarely used now. For one reason, it was extra washing when washing clothes was a hardship enough for necessities, and for another reason, no one came for dinner anymore. They knew we didn't have anything because they were in the same predicament.

Ma always wrote in her journal and then read a passage or two from her Bible just before she retired. I don't know what she would have to write in her journal nowadays as there really wasn't much that could be done or was being done. Maybe she wrote down thoughts. Whatever she wrote, I was thankful for her evening ritual, as I was able to understand so much more after having read it when she went to a better home in the sky.

"Ellen, it's time for bed," Ma said softly. "We'll go to the backhouse together. Pa has already been there and is on his way to bed."

We went out the back door to face a red sunset. The rhyme "Red sky at night, sailors delight; Red sky in the morning, sailors take warning" came to mind as we went around the corner of the house. The wind had died down to a gentle breeze. *Why can't the days be like this? I don't ever remember a dust storm at night.*

When we reached my bedroom, Ma opened the window wide and taking my blanket by its four corners, took it to the window and gave it a shake out the window to rid it of the day's dust.

"Remember to say your prayers," Ma said as she tucked me in and gave me a loving kiss on the forehead.

"I will, Ma," I said with a smile that said, "I love you".

Ellen's Story

Ma gently closed the door, and I was left alone. It still wasn't really dark yet even though it was ten o'clock of the evening. Prairie evenings are long in the summer and non-existent in the winter.

I watched the stars come on one by one. I wasn't sleepy or tired. When you don't do anything all day, how can you go to bed and sleep soundly. Pa sleeps a great deal but I don't think he is feeling well physically. The economic and weather conditions have put a great strain on him mentally, and he has a bad cough lately. Maybe it's just the dust.

The stars became brighter as night pushed the twilight away. My lazy day and my previous wanderings of my mind paved the way for more thoughts—thoughts of joy, of laughter, of sorrow, of trouble...

I was born in Tyrone County, Ireland, in the area of the northern part of Ireland where the Woods clan had been for a century. Pa was one of nine, mostly boys. A great concern of Grandpa Woods was how to divide his land among his sons so each would have enough to survive on. Pa made things a little easier by deciding to come to Canada, which we did in 1925 when I was two years old.

This I was told, and as I lay watching the stars, I tried to decipher what was actually memory and what was my imagination. Pa relished telling us stories as we sat around the big cooking range, feet on the open oven door on a cold, blustery winter night: Irish stories of the yellow gorse appearing each February to March on the surrounding hills announcing the arrival of spring; of the lambs following their mothers as they tried out their new legs, the sounds of their weak bleats when they stumbled and fell on their chins; of Grandpa's horses, the favorite work animals and pleasure horses. Pa quite frequently would pause in his narration of the horses, getting a faraway look in his eyes. Ma and I would remain silent for several minutes thinking he would continue but when he didn't we would start our own conversation or go do something else, knowing the stories were

finished for that evening. He would eventually waken from his rever-
ies, make a quick trip to the outhouse then silently climb the stairs to
his bed. On these occasions, Ma was left to bank the fire for the
night, extinguish the kerosene lamps but not before lighting a candle
that she would use to light her way to Pa's side under the feather
tick.

I understand that the Western Canadian prairies had, at the end
of the Great War, an abundance of land that had to be settled. Some
returned veterans took advantage of the cheap purchase cost, stayed,
and became prosperous. Others discovered it wasn't the kind of life
they were looking for so moved on. By the early '20's there were
some abandoned farms and still some untamed crown land that was
available to anyone, the veterans having the first choice.

Brochures reached Ireland. They showed attractive pictures of
rolling hills, plains, and coulees or small ravines covered in wild
grasses as tall as a man. Masses of blue bells and buttercups lined the
walls of the shallow and not so shallow ravines. It looked very similar
to the windswept moors of Pa's homeland. For a ridiculous low price
Pa could have five times as much land as his father owned.

Pa could see himself as lord of the manor, riding out over his
lands, his 'moors' astride a sleek fast horse, surveying the labours of
his tenants.

The brochures explained that the land was made up of parcels
called sections—640 acres but could be divided into quarters consist-
ing of 160 acres each. Advice was given that two quarters could pro-
vide a decent living for a family of four to six. These 320 acres was
more than Grandpa Woods owned that had to be divided. Pa would
own that much and more having plenty for himself and his sons he
hoped to have.

Tears would come to Ma's eyes when she told of the parting
from the family. As far as she went, it wasn't so sad. Her mother had

died giving birth to Ma after which her father had just wasted away. They say he died of a broken heart. Ma's mother's only sister took Ma to live with them even though they had a big family themselves. Ma always used to say; "I think they were glad when I left to marry your Pa as it was one less mouth to feed, especially during the war."

But Pa's family had a close relationship, and it was only the convenience of having one less offspring to be concerned about that made Pa decide to leave. Grandpa gave Pa enough money to buy the land in Canada. That was Pa's inheritance.

I don't remember how we arrived at the place we now call home, but I do know that the 10 x 12 foot shed whose door was shut, reshut, and reshut again by Mr. Wind today was where we spent our first years in this land of new customs, new weather, and new people.

CHAPTER 3

At that time of our lives, our ignorance in not knowing how bitterly cold the prairies can get made it worse. Pa had bought some coal and some wood but as it turned out, not enough. The snow would fall and the wind would blow, blocking the roads. The temperature dropped to the bottom of the thermometer, making it impossible for man or beast to travel too far.

Finally, in January a Chinook arrived. The sun warmed the shed and made everything outside a glistening white, so bright it hurt your eyes.

That first morning of the mild weather, Pa announced he was going to go to town for coal, food, and stop at our closest neighbours, the DeJongs, to see if he could buy more hay for the livestock as in that, too, he didn't buy enough.

Ma was eager to go but Pa said, "No."

"No? And pray tell, why not?" Ma exclaimed.

"Katy, me love," he said, "I don't know how long this nice weather is going to last. It could be storming and blowing by the time the sun sets again. I don't know how long I'll have to wait at the grain elevator for coal. There may be quite a line up with everyone else taking advantage of this weather. I'll get some flour and things we need and maybe a treat. The post office may have some things for us, and I'll pick up a newspaper for us to read while we tend to the stove."

"But..." Ma protested.

"Catherine." Pa was serious now. "I haven't got time to argue. It is already 8 o'clock of the morning. It's going to take at least an hour and a half to get to town what with the horses having to make their own tracks. Coming home will be slower as I'll be loaded and no doubt will walk with the horses so they don't have my weight—

which I know isn't much but it will make a difference—to pull. Besides no matter how small a fire we have in the stove now, we can't let it go out, and I'll not risk frostbite on you or our little one. Now give me a kiss, Katie, me love, and I'll be on my way."

"I guess you're right. But I did so want to go."

"I know. We've all been cooped up here for the last couple of months. Spring will soon be here, and after seeding we can start on the new house. Now, Katie," Pa said with that twinkle in his eye, "how about that kiss?"

Ma put on a brave smile, kissed him, and wished him, "God speed."

A few minutes later, we could hear the jingle of the horses' harness and Pa's hearty laugh as he made his way to town.

It was after dark when Pa finally came back to us. Ma was beginning to worry. When Pa came in after looking after the horses, he realized she had been fretting so he complimented her on looking after 'the home fires'. "That was a right thing you did, Katie, me love, to put that light in the window. This land is so flat I could see it for miles. It led me home to my two favorite girls." With a merry chuckle, he gave Ma a big hug and picked me up so I could properly give him a hug around the neck.

We were so happy to see him home. Relief set in and Ma started asking a million questions all at once.

"Hold it, Katie. I am cold and tired and hungry. How about a big bowl of that good ol' stew you have brewing on the back of the stove. After that, I will stoke the stove for the night and hit the sack. Tomorrow we will talk and go through the parcels sitting there in the corner.

The next day was like Christmas. And it was, at least for us. The real Christmas day had passed like so many of the others—to the barn to feed the livestock, back to the shed to feed ourselves and try to keep warm.

There was a parcel from Ireland—warm mufflers and mittens for everyone, letters, newspapers, and other small things that brightened up our lives. Pa was able to get a peppermint stick for me, which Ma broke into smaller pieces by giving a crack with the handle of Pa's pocketknife. Everyone then had a taste and the rest was put away in a small dish to be savored on a day when the clouds came again.

In the middle of the afternoon, Mr. DeJong came with his team and sleigh full of hay. In the evening, Ma told Pa how she and I had taken advantage of the day while he was gone to build a snowman.

Pa laughed. "Ha. Ha. And a good one it was too. He scared the living daylights out of me when I saw him last night in the moonlight." Then with a wink he said, "I didn't want my girls to know I was scared of a snowman." And then he laughed his loud and merry laugh. For a man of small stature, although he was tall, he had a good strong voice.

The next day the deep freeze set in again. After reading the newspapers, we tacked them to the walls between the studs over the others we had tacked up earlier. It helped keep the drafts at bay. Ma showed me how to make circles with her thimble on the frosted windows. By making a series of circles I could make 'stick' men or dogs or a house or whatever.

And so the days passed. Spring came. Pa ploughed a garden spot for Ma, her first in the new country. Then he went to work on his first fifty acres.

He would come in when he could no longer see, tired but jubilant.

"Katie, me love. This is a great country. We are going to make our fortune here. Now that the first fifty acres are seeded, I'll start breaking another fifty. Next year, I'll be able to seed one hundred acres. That is as much as my father owns, and he has to divide it up. Yes, sir. We made a wise choice coming here. I'm my own boss, and I have enough land to share it with my sons you're going to give me. Katie, me love, I'm so glad we came to Canada." To show his pleasure, he kissed Ma and lifted me up above his head and made me giggle. His booming, joyful sound that habitually came from his throat, filled the rafters of the little shed we called home.

CHAPTER 4

As I said, spring came and so did the DeJongs, all seven of them. Horace and Zelda, the parents; Lisa and Marie, twelve and thirteen years old respectively; Andrew was nine, Peter was five and Olga was my age. She had just turned three in January. I wouldn't be three years old until June. Years later, when Olga and I became good friends, she would tease me when we had a friendly dispute. She would say, " Listen to your elders." This would set us to laughing.

Mr. DeJong had come a few times last fall to help Pa set up the stove in the shed, to help fix up the old barn good enough to shelter the one cow and the horses, and to haul the hay Pa had bought from him. He couldn't help much more as he had his crop to harvest and to make his own place ready for winter. Pa had asked his advice about how much coal, wood, and hay he needed. Mr. DeJong thought we had enough for a usual winter, but if it was to be a 'doozy of a winter', we would be short.

As it turned out—as has been told—it was a 'doozy' of a winter. When Mr. DeJong brought the extra hay during the warm spell, he was all apologies. To compensate, he dropped the price of the hay. Pa heartily shook hands with Mr. DeJong declaring, "I am so glad we came to Canada."

This declaration was made over and over again during the course of the first six years we lived in our new country.

When the DeJong family came, it was early spring. There was still little bits of dirty snow in places where the sun didn't go, but Pa was able to plough Ma's little garden patch. Spring rains would break down the big lumps of overturned sod further. This would make it easier for Ma to work the ground with her hoe and rake. Ma proudly showed Zelda—I mean Mrs. DeJong—and the girls the spot, asking advice as to when to plant certain plants.

Ellen's Story

"Well, Catherine," said Mrs. DeJong. "Plant your potatoes first around Queen Victoria's birthday which is May 24. I don't think I have to tell an Irish woman to plant a good many." They both chuckled at the little joke on how Irish people like their potatoes. "Then carrots and turnips followed by…"

"Turnips," interrupted Ma. "Isn't that cow fodder?"

Mrs. DeJong smiled. "I made that same exclamation when I was told to plant turnips. That was thirteen years ago. Back home in Holland we also used turnips for the few cattle that exist. But they were a different kind of turnip. Get the Rutabaga kind with the purple top. They are sweet and delicious and winter well. Sally, at the general store in town, can help you buy your seeds. They will be on the shelves soon."

They went on talking about gardening and other things while Pa, Mr. DeJong, and the boys looked over Pa's fifty acres that was still too wet to do anything with. Mr. DeJong offered the use of his own disc after he was finished using it. His land was pretty dry and would be able to be worked next week. That would give Pa plenty of time to do his field and still get the wheat planted in time. They continued talking about farming with Mr. DeJong warning Pa not to get too carried away with his fencing.

"After all, Mr. Woods, you…"

"Kelly's the name," Pa interrupted and extended his hand to Mr. DeJong. And if I may call you Horace?"

"Oh, but definitely," he said as he grasped Pa's hand. "As I was saying you only have a cow and a couple of horses."

"But I'm going to have fifty head of cattle and at least ten horses," Pa boasted.

"Like I was saying, go slow. Cattle costs money…" They continued with the pros and cons of buying too much or too few cattle un-

21

til Ma called Pa to get the fire going for coffee as it was lunchtime and everyone needed to be fed.

Pa immediately did as he was asked. Ma walked with her new neighbour/lady friend to her wagon. Mrs. DeJong took out a huge basket of cold chicken and ham, home made bread, pickles, cookies, and cake.

"We hope you won't be offended by us bringing the food. We thought it best, as you weren't expecting us. Being such a beautiful day we thought we would make a celebration out of meeting our new neighbours. Spring house-cleaning has been done. There's not much that can be done yet in the fields or yard so now is a good time for a picnic and a holiday," Mrs. DeJong announced all this with a smile ending with her infectious little giggle.

Of course, Pa gave his hearty ha-ha and his declaration that all was merry at the Wood's primitive but promising homestead.

Ma laid out a couple of heavy blankets on the grass where it was warm and dry. This was on the south side of the shed. Pa and Mr. DeJong carried out the table with Peter and Andrew struggling with the three chairs. Pa found a good stump from the woodpile for him to sit on.

Lisa and Marie helped us younger kids with our meal as we all sat together on the quilts. Olga and I sat close together. We didn't say much, but Olga had inherited her mother's giggle and used it from time to time.

After the lunch, things were cleared away and Olga and I had had our nap on the quilts in the warmth of the spring sun, Mrs. De-Jong told Ma to grab a pillow case or sack of some sort, "Because we're going dandelion hunting."

"Whatever for?" declared Ma.

"The new tender dandelion greens make the most delicious veg-etable, something akin to spinach only better. The blossoms make good wine but since we don't indulge we let them bloom and wither. The greens also make a good salad, as does chickweed. But if you ever get chickweed in your garden..." Mrs. DeJong chattered on as we made our way to the coulee that split the prairie like a crack in a chocolate cake that rose too fast in the oven. The men and boys went off hunting gophers and Jack rabbits with their .22's.

The hunt was successful. The DeJongs refused to stay for supper using fatigue as their excuse. Inwardly, I think Ma was just as glad as she was quite tired herself. She cooked up most of the greens while Pa skinned a rabbit, stretched it out, and nailed the hide to the side of the barn. It was still chilly at night so we kept the stove going and put the rabbit on the top to stew all night. It would be tomorrow's supper.

Before retiring for the night, we took advantage of the quilts that were still outside on the grass. Ma and Pa sat with their backs leaning on the shed walls. I crawled up on Ma's lap. I was still a very small child, thin like Pa so I was able to cuddle up quite nicely. We sat there a long while as we watched the sun go down in a blaze of pink and purple glory accented by lavender tinted fluffy clouds. Pa was quiet for once. Ma left him to his contemplating. It was such a peaceful time, so soothing, so restful, and as I fell asleep on Ma's lap, I wondered why her tummy was so hard.

CHAPTER 5

It wasn't long after that eventful day that we woke to the sound of raindrops pitter-pattering on the roof.

"Ah, Katie, me love, isn't that just the most wonderful sound? Sounds like money in the bank. Makes a fella want to stay in bed and dream," Pa said as he lazily stretched his lean body.

Ma was up gathering pots and dishpans, still in her nightgown. Between quick burst outside to leave the pots under the eves to catch the rain, she answered Pa by saying, "You can dream after chores are done as there won't be much else to do."

"Right you are, Katie, me love." As he was going out the door, Ma called to him. "Before you come back in, take down the wash tubs from the shed wall and put them under the eves, too, please."

About a half hour later we could hear Pa doing as he was asked. Coming inside, he exclaimed, "Whatever are we going to do with all the water you're catching?"

"I am going to wash the sheets and curtains. Then we all are going to have a bath, and you are going to keep the fire going so that the sheets will be dry by the time we go to bed this evening."

"Ah, but Katie, that will keep me busy all day. I won't have time for dreaming."

Ma looked at him to see if he was serious. She saw the twinkle in his eye.

It was a busy day, but we were able to put clean bodies between clean sheets. The rain on the roof did its share in getting us to sleep.

In a few days, the rain stopped. We stepped from our shelter to survey a bright shiny wet world. The garden plot was a maze of mountains and rivers. Pa proposed a walk. With rubber boots getting larger with each step across the yard we finally made it to the prairie grass and the edge of the coulee. Before we proceeded down the long slope to the water that rippled and gurgled over the rocks of the coulee bottom, Pa stood and gazed over the land that was his, the 320 acres. He could visualize a hundred horses grazing on part of the land while hay as tall as a man swayed in the wind like the ocean that we had just recently crossed. He was quiet for quite a while. Suddenly, the spell was broke by Pa's hearty laugh. "Yes, Katie, me love, this is a great country."

The hot prairie sun worked its wonders, and before long, Ma was in the garden with spade, hoe, and rake preparing it for seed while Pa rode the disc behind the two powerful grey Percherons as he prepared the field for oats.

Sally at the general store proved to be a big help with the garden seeds, and soon both garden and fields were planted. Nothing more to do with them but let Mother Nature take her course.

Dianne Osborne

CHAPTER 6

Pa was not a real ambitious man. He could work hard when a project had to be done, working at it whole-heartedly. He had spent some long hours behind the horses now he could spend a few lazy days telling Ma his dreams. She listened patiently as she had heard them all winter long.

Pa's next project was digging a well. He rose early each morning digging with such swiftness you would think he planned to have it all dug before the sun set that night.

Periodically, Ma would bring him a jug of water from the rain barrel on the north side of the shed where the water was still cool from the absence of the sun. Pa would drink gustily then give Ma a kiss on the forehead declaring, "Katie, me love, you are just like this cool drink of water–refreshing. And especially because you've started to blossom again since we've come here."

Ma blushed. "Oh, Pa." was all she could say.

The next day, Pa required Ma's help. He was down far enough where bracing and timbers were needed to keep the walls of dirt from caving in. Ma would slide the timber to the edge until Pa could grab hold of them and place them where he needed them. By evening, he was digging again, filling pails and winding them up. Ma would take the pails of dirt and empty them away from the well hole. A couple of times she had to stop, as a pain in her side would make her bend over. A look of pain on her face quickly disappeared when she noticed me watching her. I wasn't very old. I thought she had a tummy ache.

By mid-morning the next day, that 'tummy ache' caused Ma to collapse to the ground with a groan.

I ran to her and said, "Me help you up."

26

Ellen's Story

Ma tried to smile and managed to whisper, "Pa will have to help me. Go to the well and call him."

As I left her side, she warned, "Be careful of the edge."

"Pa," I yelled from about three feet from the edge.

"What is it, Sprig?"

"Ma has a bad tummy ache," I answered.

"What makes you think that?"

"She's falled down by the dirt."

Pa was out of that hole in about two seconds flat making it o her side in two strides of his long legs.

"Katie! Katie! What's wrong?"

"I hurt, Kelly. Maybe you should get Mrs. DeJong."

He jumped to his feet, white of face and exclaiming, "Of course, of course." He took a few quick steps this way then a few quick steps back knowing he had to do something in a hurry but not knowing really what he should do. Seeing me standing helpless and close to tears, decisions came clear.

"Ellen, honey, you go in the house and get Ma her pillow and a blanket off the bed. Bring it to Ma. I have to go get Mrs. DeJong.

He whistled for Marty, the Morgan riding horse, and as she trotted into the yard, he grabbed her mane, swinging easily up on her back. He was off at a gallop.

It seemed like hours before Pa came back even though it probably was a very short time. But to a four-year-old sitting beside her very sick Mother, time passed agonizingly slow. Soon after, Mr. and Mrs. DeJong came in their wagon.

Mrs. DeJong took over, telling the men to do this, do that, and after she had Ma settled in bed she came to me and asked, "Would you like to come home with me and sleep at our house with Olga in her big bed?"

Not quite understanding, I stammered "Ma...Pa..."

"Your Ma and Pa are going to stay here. It would be like a holiday for you. Olga will like sharing her room and her dolls."

I looked at Pa. He had a smile on his face. "Go, Sprig. Have some fun. Ma is sick right now so it's no fun to be here."

In my mind, I thought that if Ma is sick, I want to be with her. But they all seemed to want me to go. With heavy heart, I allowed them to roll my nightgown and a few personal things and hand me into the wagon beside Mrs. DeJong. She put her arm around me and held me close making me feel more secure. As we began to leave, Pa came running up to the wagon with my rag doll from Ireland. I hugged her close and thought, *"I guess everything is going to be alright."*

A few days later Pa came for me riding Marty bareback. He did take time for a bit and reins, but for Pa to feel the flesh and movement of a horse beneath him was the ultimate joy.

Pa sat me in front of him using one strong arm to hold me close to him, the other to hold the reins. Pa's movements coincided with the horse's movements as if they were one. I enjoyed the ride and many other rides with Pa as long as his arm was around me. In later years, Pa would put me on the horse by myself, slowly and explicitly giving me instructions. But without his arm around me, I froze. I was afraid to ride alone. I would cry, pleading to be let down. When Pa lifted me to the ground, it was with a sad face. Immediately, he would mount Marty and off they would gallop. They would be gone for hours.

I know I was a disappointment to him when it came to horses. But somehow without Pa, I just couldn't bring myself to make the horse move.

The next day Pa went into town on Marty, but this time he used a saddle as he also took the saddlebags. Some provisions were needed, and he was also going to check the mail.

Ellen's Story

He was gone all day. It was my bedtime and still no Pa. But at breakfast there sat Pa at the table smiles all over his face and eyes twinkling as he took from the saddle bags placed in the corner the night before, three fresh oranges.

"Pa," Ma exclaimed, "wherever did you find money to buy these?"

Pa laughed. "Katie, me love, never underestimate my ability to shop. I had a few pennies left, and I found a nickel on the sidewalk so I spent them on this treat."

Ma didn't laugh. She just looked at him.

Pa saw the look and put his arm around her saying, "Don't worry about it, Katie, me love. It wasn't much."

After breakfast, Pa went back to digging the well that he had neglected for the last few days. Mr. DeJong came to help and by evening there was water in the well. There was still work to be done on the well, but Pa was happy. The water was good water, and there was lots of it.

And life became normal again.

CHAPTER 7

Pa didn't get the house started that summer. Soon after the well was operational, it was time for hay to be cut and stored in the loft of the barn. Pa helped Mr. DeJong with his hay; in return, Mr. DeJong cut Pa's hay, as Pa didn't have a mower. We borrowed Mr. DeJong's hay rack and the three of us brought our own hay in. Ma and Pa would pitch it into the rack with forks. When I was older, it was my job to tramp it down so we could bring in a bigger load.

How sweet it smelled. And to ride on top on the way in from the field was like riding on a magic carpet. I could see the trees in the creek and the bushes at the end of it. I could see DeJong's yard a mile away. I could see the neighbours' wheat fields (still green) swaying in the wind reminding me of a great green sea. And over all this was a big blue bowl of endless sky. Sometimes it was decorated with white streaks, other times it was clear blue.

The odd time there were dark brooding storm clouds on the distant horizon. Although they were miles away, the prairie wind was capable of bringing them overhead in a short time. At this time, Ma and Pa pitched like crazy, and I trampled in the same manner—then the wild ride just ahead of the rain, right into the barn. No time for unloading until skies were clear again.

After Mr. DeJong's hay and ours was done, Pa helped other neighbours and they would pay him. When Pa didn't have to help the following day, he would be late coming home from the neighbours he had been helping. Sometimes the next morning there would be a treat for us.

"Paid me a little extra, that man did, Katie, me love." Then he would wink at her and give her a quick hug.

Ellen's Story

Ma never seemed to be happy about it. She was even sadder when Pa came home late and told us the next morning that another neighbour hadn't paid so much.

Ma would sit down with elbows on the table, her face in her hands and shake her head as if to say, "No, don't let me hear that."

Pa would put his arm around her shoulders and try to comfort her by saying, "Don't take it so hard, Katie, me love. He didn't short change me that much."

When he could, Pa would jump on Marty and take off on his own generally following the creek. Most of the time he was gone all day. What he did we don't know. He didn't say anymore than he had to on those days, and when a word was spoken, it was done gruffly. It was like an invisible wall was built up around him. We couldn't reach him so we stopped trying. Thank goodness, those moods would last only a day or two at the most.

Then came harvest. Pa again was a willing hand on the threshing crew that went from farm to farm. Before the crew came to our place, Pa had bought some planks to make tables and benches. Mrs. DeJong came to help Ma bake pies and cook big pots of potatoes and vegetables. Her oldest daughters kept us smaller one occupied and out of the way. Counting the DeJong family, us and the crew there were at least twenty mouths that had to be fed for three or four days, each day three times plus coffee and goodies in between meals. It was a busy time, but exciting.

It was exciting to watch the straw stack grow higher and higher until it stood on the south side of the barn, protected by the north wind, glowing in the sun like a pile of gold out of the fairy tale story book Ma read to me at night.

But we were not to touch that stack of gold. If we did, bad things would happen. Just like a curse. We had to satisfy ourselves to just stand and look in awe at what we thought was a whole lot of fun

Dianne Osborne

just going to waste. We knew from other experiences that we must
obey our parents.

CHAPTER 8

We spent another winter in the shed. Pa started the new house in the spring after the crop was in. It was only half the house built that way due to lack of finances. The purchase of livestock was more important and, of course, his beloved horses came first. He had two Percherons for fieldwork and a Morgan for riding or for pulling the small wagon we used for traveling back and forth to town five miles away.

Being only half a house, the roof had only slope to the south. The chimney rose outside the north wall in the center. When the house was to be completed, the chimney would be in the middle of the house, the thought being that one stove could heat all the downstairs rooms—there would be four of them—while a hole with a grate in the ceiling in the kitchen area would let the heat rise to the upper rooms.

It really wasn't a good-looking house at this stage. A porch was built on the west end. The front door on the south had a big flat stone for a door step which was bleached white by the sun and washed sparkling clean by the rain. Ma tried to make it look pleasant by planting some flowers on either side of the rock but the sun reflecting off the new white boards of the house, the sun itself, and the dry soil, caused by the ever-present wind, soon killed the plants.

As I said, it wasn't much to look at, but it was a far cry from the shed where we spent our first two winters.

While helping Pa with the construction of the new house, Ma had another 'spell' with pains in her stomach that sent me back to the DeJongs again for a day or two. Mrs. DeJong felt Ma should take it easier so Ma got out her crochet hook and thread along with her needle and embroidery thread and proceeded to create doilies, runner scarves, afghans, etc. to decorate her new home.

Crops were good that year. Cows, pigs, and chickens were added giving us fresh eggs, bacon, and milk. Ma's garden produced well filling up many sealers. The abundant wild berries—saskatoons, strawberries and blue berries—filled up more sealers.

We were a small but happy family. We became acquainted with a few more people who occasionally came for Sunday dinner. DeJongs were the most frequent quests and usually the ones who invited us back. Looking back in my more mature years, I could see that Pa's loud laugh and endless story telling made a person wonder what was truth and what was not, was not tolerated too well by the quiet prairie people. Mr. DeJong tolerated Pa. Maybe because his wife always seemed to enjoy Pa's stories. At least she laughed and giggled a great deal.

Pa did love to tell stories. Many a long winter evening, he kept Ma and me entertained. For Ma it was repetition, having heard them many times before. When we moved into the new house, Pa moved his stories in with us telling them over again as we sat in the kitchen gathered around the cooking range, our feet resting on the opened oven door.

One such night as we sat around the stove the wind started to roar in the chimney. Or so we thought. Suddenly, Pa stopped talking in mid-sentence. Quiet for only a second to determine whether his hearing was right or not, he suddenly leaped to his feet crying, "Catherine, grab the basin of water."

Ma was oblivious of the noise in the chimney. I often thought that her mind was miles away when Pa started on his story telling. This night seemed to verify my suspicions.

She calmly sat in her rocking chair and ignorantly asked, "Whatever for?"

"Woman," Pa shouted at her, "can't you hear the roar in the chimney? We have a fire in there."

Ma's eyes grew large. She came into motion in a useless manner almost to the point of panicking.

Pa grabbed his leather sheep-skinned lined mitts. He lifted the stovepipe from the stove and yelled, "Put that God-damned basin under the pipe."

Ma finally got the message and did as she was told.

"Now I need your bag of salt," Pa ordered.

"Salt. I need that for cooking."

You could see that Pa was beginning to lose his patience. "Give me the salt," he said pronouncing each word distinctly.

Reluctantly, Ma gave him the two-pound bag of salt.

Without grabbing a jacket, he hurried outside to the north side of the house. Here he scrambled up the ladder that Mr. DeJong advised him to build onto the house.

"Your roof has got a fair good slope on it. If you happen to get a chimney fire—and they do happen—you'll be needing it to reach the peak and your chimney," Mr. DeJong had told Pa. No doubt, Pa was glad he had listened.

In a few minutes, he was back inside announcing all was well. He didn't reprimand Ma for her slowness or her unwillingness to follow orders. He just gave her an unkind look and shook his head. There was no more conversation between them for the rest of the evening.

After all was over, Pa went out to the barn. Here he wrapped a gunnysack around a big stone and tied all to a small rope. Ascending the ladder once more, he ran the ball of rock and gunnysack up and down the chimney. When he was satisfied it was clean enough, he returned to the house, lit the stove, and advised us it was time for bed.

Ma obediently went upstairs taking me with her. I guess the look she had received from Pa was enough to tell her he was not pleased with her.

35

Pa stayed up for awhile until he was happy with the performance of the stove. After banking the firebox for the night he too came up the stairs.

Right after chores the next day Pa rode into town on Marty. The weather was not that nice so he didn't stay long, fearful of a sudden storm. Upon returning, he strode into the house and plunked a two-pound bag of salt on the table.

"Here's your salt," He declared. "I'll be in the barn. I'll return when I'm ready." He walked out before she could answer.

CHAPTER 9

The year I was six Ma started to put on weight again. As she grew larger, Pa became more and more excited and more and more considerate in helping her with this and that, not letting her lift anything nor letting her walk too far. By September, when I was about to start school, Ma could only waddle so Pa walked with me to the DeJongs. From there Olga, Peter, and Andrew would take me to the one room schoolhouse that was another mile down the road. In the afternoon, Pa would be waiting for me at the DeJongs' gate, sometimes with the horse.

One day Pa wasn't there. Only a note for Andrew to walk me home. As we reached the house, we saw Pa rush out the back door with what looked like a bundle of soiled cloth. He stopped at the shed for a shovel and headed for the small grove of trees he had planted north of the house. Mrs. DeJong caught us watching him dig a hole and put the bundle into it. He then covered it with the dirt from the hole.

"Oh, dear." I heard her mumble under her breath in an agitated way. "What bad timing."

Then turning to Andrew and me, she cheerfully said, "I'm sorry I made you walk all this way, but I didn't realize your Ma was so sick when your Pa called for me."

Before she could continue, I burst into tears. Ma was sick. She needed me. I started for the house.

Mrs. DeJong gently grabbed my arm and held me close. I remember her pleasant smelling floral perfume. (Pa always bought Ma such strong stuff.) "Ellen, sweetheart," she said, "your Ma needs lots of rest. Andrew will take you back to our place. It will be like a holiday for you." I didn't want to go, but I always enjoyed myself when I was there.

I stayed a week this time. When I returned, Ma was still quite weak and very thin. Pa hardly spoke. Ma didn't encourage him for fear of the gruff answer she might get.

Time and necessary chores have a way of smoothing things out. By Thanksgiving, in the middle of October, the crop and garden were all in the granary and sealers putting Pa in a good mood.

"Well, Katie, me love," he boomed on that festive weekend, "the crops gave me a good dollar. I think I'll go after one of my dreams by going into the city to do some horse dealing." He gave her a broad wink.

"No, Kelly, No!" Ma was horrified. At that time, I couldn't understand why Ma was stopping Pa from having one of his dreams come true. No amount of persuasion could deter Pa from going. He had made up his mind. As he started to leave, he put both hands on her shoulders and looked straight into her eyes. He said, "Remember Cork, Katy. Remember Cork," and he was gone.

Ma crumbled into a nearby chair and cried into her apron. Ma had been sick and now she was sad. My little mind was confused as to what was really happening. It all made me feel sad too.

Pa came back a few days later all excited and bearing gifts for us. He couldn't talk fast enough to get out all he had to tell. I caught the words 'long term investments' (whatever that was) and he ended with "The short term investments let me buy this beautiful fur shawl for the best woman in the world, the one I love with all my heart."

Ma was speechless as he wrapped a light brown mink stole around her shoulders.

"But–but...where and when would I ever wear such a beautiful thing, Kelly?" Ma stammered.

"We will attend the New Year's Eve shindig in town and show all those ladies with their noses in the air just who we really are." He let one of his loud laughs bounce off the kitchen walls.

Ellen's Story

For me, there was a beautifully dressed baby doll with eyes that closed and opened. She came to be a very special possession in the years to come.

Pa's good mood only lasted ten days. Listening to the news on the battery radio on the morning of Black Friday, Oct. 29, 1929, Pa drew out a string of oaths so long and loud Ma had to clamp her hand over his mouth and admonish him by saying, "Kelly, we do have a small child in the home."

Grabbing his coat and hat from the peg by the door, Pa left, slamming the door with a loud bang. We didn't see him for two days. We don't know where he went, and, as usual, we didn't ask.

And again as usual when he returned so had his good nature. There was nothing unusual about the way he hollered, "Hey, Katie, me love, I'm home," as he removed his coat and hat and replaced them on the peg. After a hug from a quiet but relieved Ma, he tugged at my waist-length pigtails and tapped my freckled nose with his forefinger while saying, "How's my girl Sprig?"

Nothing was said about his absence. For days, Pa went about his usual outside chores and as the evenings were getting long, the fireside stories began. If he faltered, a request for a particular story would be voiced.

On New Year's Eve day, Pa talked constantly, a sign that told us he was excited. His face was full of smiles as he placed the mink stole over Ma's shoulders that evening as they prepared for the New Year's Eve frolic.

They went with the DeJongs in their car while I stayed with Olga, Peter, and the rest. As usual, I enjoyed myself. However, I wasn't so sure about Ma and Pa.

I was sleeping when they arrived back at DeJongs so they just picked up blankets and all to take me home. The next day, Pa did his chores and Ma prepared a pleasant New Year's Day dinner for the three of us. Not a word was said about what anyone had thought or said about Ma's fur piece. Knowing a small community's reputation for snobbery among the upper crust, they probably ignored Ma more with her fur than if she hadn't had it at all. After all, it was worn over her cloth coat that was beginning to show signs of wear at the cuffs, down the front, and at the pockets.

Ma hung her 'moment of glory' on a hanger in the upper closet. The incident was never mentioned again.

CHAPTER 10

The following Sunday, the DeJongs came for dinner. After dishes were done, the adults fell to playing cards while we youngsters bundled up to go outside. We wanted to try out Peter's new sled.

New snow had fallen and had built up some drifts in the creek. With great anticipation of sledding all afternoon, we made our way to the rim. Peter threw his sled down at the beginning of what was to be our sled run first taking hold of the rope to keep it from going down on its own.

The most dreadful sound and sight to an excited group of would-be sledders was the thud the metal runners made as they sank up to the boards into soft snow.

"We need some water," Andrew quickly surmised being he was at least ten years old and so much wiser than the rest of us.

"Where are we going to get water when every thing is frozen?" Peter argued.

All were quiet until I remembered Ma's rain barrel by the stove in the kitchen in readiness for tomorrow's washing of clothes.

"Ma has her water in the barrel to wash clothes with tomorrow. But maybe we shouldn't use it."

"Oh, we won't need much," Andrew asserted.

I gave in. I found a pail, and Andrew, being the tallest, quietly went into the kitchen to help himself to a pail of water from Ma's supply.

The adults were in the far room getting excited about their card game. The first couple of times we entered the house we weren't noticed. When we were noticed, Pa called from his chair at the card table, "What do you kids need?"

I stammered, "We're just getting a little bit of water to make some ice."

"Oh, okay. Have fun." Pa chuckled.

When we went back out, I said, "I don't think we'd better take anymore." The rest agreed. We were discovering that it was going to take more than Ma's wash water to make a smooth icy sled run.

We stayed outside for a while longer, but since we had slopped water not only on the snow but on us too, we soon became cold and chilly.

Trooping noisily into the kitchen, we were still able to hear Mr. DeJong say, "Well, Zelda, we had better run along home. There's chores to do before this afternoon light disappears."

"Yes, Horace, both you and Kelly have chores to do. It's been such a pleasant day, Katie. Thank you for the lovely day. I must get that recipe for that desert. It was simply delicious," said Zelda with a giggle.

By now, everyone was in the kitchen. Ma pushed the kettle closer to the front of the stove in readiness for our own evening meal when she noticed the half empty rain barrel.

"What happened to my water?" she exclaimed.

No one said a word, but eyes were moving. Pa said, "Sprig, was that the 'little bit of water' you needed for ice?"

I could only nod my head in the affirmative.

Again silence. Finally, Andrew spilled the beans and told all.

Mr. and Mrs. DeJong scolded their eldest son, and he apologized to Ma and Pa. I thought he was very nice about it, but since it really was my idea to use that water I gulped and finally sputtered out, "I'm sorry, Ma."

All of a sudden, Pa's roar of laughter let loose and nearly frightened every one out of their wits. Pa saw the funny side of it. "Don't—Ha, Ha—don't you kids worry about it. There's more snow outside. Ha. Ha."

Ellen's Story

"Well, yes, there is, Kelly," Mr. DeJong agreed. "But now more has to be brought in. Come get on your coat and I'll help you. So will my boys." He looked at each one of them as if to say, "It's partly your fault."

It didn't take long to refill the barrel. The DeJongs left with no hard feelings. It was all part of prairie life.

But it wasn't so funny in the morning. I was cold, and then I was hot, then back to cold. I hurt all over and was dizzy a bit as I slowly descended the stairs in my nightgown and socks. I had trouble keeping my eyes open yet I was awake.

Ma took one look at me and exclaimed, "My dear child, you have a fever. By the look of your red cheeks it must be a high one."

She ran upstairs for a quilt and the thermometer she kept in the medicine 'shoe' box. Returning, she wrapped me in the quilt and placed me in the rocking chair pulling it close to the already hot cooking range. The thermometer, after being under my tongue for a minute or so, proved I had, indeed, a very high fever.

Ma, continuing in her role as my personal nurse, then crushed half of an adult Bayer aspirin between two spoons and made me eat it. Yuk, but that stuff tastes terrible. Even a glass of warm milk to wash it down still left a bitter taste on my tongue.

When Pa came in from doing chores, Ma told him of my condition. Immediately, he came to the side of the rocking chair and knelt there looking into my hot flushed face with his own face full of worry and concern.

"Well, my little Sprig," he said gently, "this doesn't look so good."

I couldn't answer him. The warmth of the quilt and stove and the aspirin were starting to work their wonders. I was getting very drowsy.

Pa straightened and then leaned over picking quilt and me up into his arms. He settled his lean lanky body into the rocking chair nestling my head onto his shoulder. That's where we stayed till evening chores. Ma quietly interrupted at noon with hot turkey broth for both of us. My throat was too sore to get much down.

Through the long winter evening Pa and I rocked, even on into the night, until Ma became concerned for Pa.

"Kelly, you need some rest too. We can't have you getting run down. She'll be all right in her bed. I'll check her through the night."

"No offense, Katie, dear. I know you mean well, but I'm not about to lose this child. I'll be all right. You go to bed. You'll need to feed us on the morrow."

Ma leaned over and kissed his brow and then mine. She climbed the stairs with a candle.

I had just witnessed one of the very rare moments of gentle happiness between Ma and Pa.

CHAPTER 11

Had there been school, I would have missed two weeks. For three days, I wandered in and out of the living world. Relief from the burning up sensation came after Ma spooned down the crushed half of a Bayer aspirin and tipped hot tea into my parched throat. Cold compresses on my forehead cooled me off somewhat, allowing me to fall asleep again on Pa's shoulders.

On the fourth morning, I woke when Pa handed me to Ma so she could keep me warm while Pa did the chores. And I was still awake when he came back into the house. I felt tired but cooled down.

"It looks like the fever has broken, Pa," Ma said.

Pa felt my face and looked into my eyes and said, "Welcome back, my little Sprig. You sure had us worried these last few days."

I still sat by the stove, but I was able to get dressed. In the afternoon, Pa and I had our snooze in the rocking chair. After ten days I was back to normal.

There was no need for me to go back to school. The bottom of the thermometer dropped out. For the whole month of January it never reached above -30°F during the day. To heat the one roomed clapboard schoolhouse in such cold weather wasn't feasible.

I wasn't the only one who cuddled up to the big black cooking range. Pa was so glad to have me back among the land of the living that he talked incessantly, planning what we would do in the spring, next winter, and on and on and on. Ma, sitting close to get her fair share of the heat, admonished him by saying, "You'll play our Sprig out by just talking about it."

This brought out a chuckle and a squeeze for me.

Not only was it cold but also the wind would blow giving a wind chill of well below –40°F. One morning, Pa returned from the barn with milk all over his pant legs.

"Did you fall, Pa?" Ma asked when she saw it.

"No, Ma. That wind is so strong and gusty that it just scooped the milk out of the pail and all over me. I'm lucky I have some left." He showed her a half empty pail. "I'll need a cloth or some kind of cover for the pail if this wind keeps up."

On calm days, there would be a skiff of ice on the top of the milk by the time Pa came into the house.

The Chinook came at the beginning of February. Eagerly, we returned to school to our newfound friends.

Of course, my closest friends were Olga, Peter, and Andrew. Olga had her mother's infectious giggle causing even me, who was a bit shy and quiet, to burst out into laughter. Sometimes, Olga and I would roll on the ground howling over some little thing that really wasn't funny, but it had tickled our funny bones.

Peter thought we were stupid when we got into one of our fits, but Andrew just smiled and let us have our way.

As much as I 'loved' Olga and her merry ways, I was always glad to sit quietly with Peter. He was two years older than me and so much more wiser even at the age of eight.

Even the adults of our two families enjoyed each other's company. It was cards or checkers in the winter exchanging houses and then picnics and berry picking in the summer. Of course, everybody came on those excursions even the two older DeJong girls when they could. They had already finished their grade eight and had moved on to 'another life.'

CHAPTER 12

Pa worked for Mr. DeJong in exchange for the use of some of Mr. DeJong's machinery. Many times, Pa also got a few dollars. With the stock market crash of 1929, Pa had to become more serious about his land. The near loss of me sobered him a great deal, and he began to understand sentimental feelings more. He accepted me as a girl now. I had the feeling he was quite happy to have me alive, not caring whether or not I could ride a horse on my own. We two became closer. In fact, all three of us became more conscious of one and other. This closeness of ours could also have been cause by the tragedy that occurred in the DeJong family.

It was in the spring, two years after my battle with the fever. Pa was helping the DeJongs prepare for seeding. This one particular night he didn't get home until after dark. He looked as if the world had ended. I guess, for the DeJongs, it had.

He shooed me out of Ma's rocking chair and sat down in it. He pulled me up on his lap, put his arm around my shoulder, and my head on his shoulder.

"Katie, dear, come pull a chair close to us. I have a terrible story to tell. Maybe it might be too much for Sprig, but I think she's old enough to understand."

Ma put a couple more sticks of wood in the stove. The spring nights were still cool and a warm fire was a welcome comfort.

When all was ready, Pa began, "Horace—that's Mr. DeJong to you, Sprig—is a very good farmer, and he is teaching his boys to be good farmers too. Peter is still a little young for the big stuff but Andrew,"—here Pa choked on his name then swallowed hard before continuing—"Andrew was very good with the horses and plough. He was strong enough to handle both, and his fondness for the animals made it easier for him to work with them.

47

Well, Andrew was out ploughing today. Did you girls get caught in that sudden rain storm today?" Pa asked, temporarily changing the subject. Thinking of this incident in later years he probably changed the subject to give himself time to think how he could go on with his terrible tale.

I piped up and said, "Yes, Ma had to run to take a few things off the line."

Ma continued my story, "Just as I was reaching the steps with my arms full of clothes there came such a loud clap of thunder it nearly scared me out of my wits."

Pa never cracked a smile. On another occasion, Ma's incident might have been comical but not this time.

"Yes, well, Andrew was out in the field when the storm hit. He was able to get the horses to the shelter of the tree belt. He stood in front of them, holding their heads to keep them quiet. Both Horace and I ran to the shelter to give him a hand, and as we ran that thunderclap that scared you out of your wits also scared the horses. Andrew was not strong enough to hold them. They bolted. We saw, as we ran, Andrew being knocked down and the plough starting to over him. The horses stopped then, and when we reached Andrew, we saw why."

Here Pa stopped talking to bite his lips and close his eyes, fighting to keep the tears in.

Huskily, he began again, "Horace and I had to pull the plough shears from Andrew's hip." Pa let the tears stream down his face.

Only the soft singing of the kettle on the stove and the ticking of the kitchen clock were heard in the deafening silence that enveloped us.

There was no stopping the tears so Pa continued, "Horace picked Andrew up as if he was a child and carried him through the shelterbelt and on up to the house. I unhooked the plough and took the horses to the barn where I unharnessed them and put them in their stalls.

"When I reached the house, Andrew had been laid on the floor by the stove. Zelda was calmly trying to soak up the blood with towels. I'm sure they were both dying inside but they are the kind of people who are capable of keeping their heads when certain jobs have to be done.

"Someone had called the doctor. By the time he arrived, Andrew was barely alive and delirious. He was repeating the Lord's Prayer and when he got to 'Thy will be done' he slipped away from us.

"While the doctor consoled the grieving parents, I went out to see to the horses; they needed to be rubbed down and fed. Then I saw to the rest of the chores. I went to the house to tell them all was ready for the night. By this time the doctor had left taking Andrew's body, and the floor had been washed clean of his blood.

Horace hugged me and I hugged him back. He said the funeral would be tomorrow afternoon around 2 o'clock at the farm. They've decided on a nice little sheltered spot by the trees for the burial. I volunteered to help dig the hole tomorrow morning."

Ma whispered, "I'll make up some squares for lunch."

And then we all hugged each other. Pa laid his cheek on the top of my head and cried. Ma said the Lord's Prayer emphasizing 'Thy will be done' and then stopped. Pa crossed himself.

A few neighbours came to the funeral. Ma had put black ribbons—maybe it was seam binding—in my pigtails even though it was unheard of for a child to wear black. But she wanted people to know that the three of us mourned the death of Andrew, the son who was shaping up to be the future farmer, who was a great source of pride to his father. Mr. DeJong had no less love or pride for Peter, but Peter was thin and seemed to be more interested in books. No doubt he would do well for himself in the future, but Andrew was the farmer, the real inheritor.

After the service and the dirt replaced in the hole, Pa and Mr. DeJong embraced again. They held onto each other and cried like two children. No one chided them; they just lowered their heads and walked calmly up to the house leaving Pa and Mr. DeJong to themselves.

Ma took up the job of hostess. Before we left we made sure that all was clean in the house and all were fed in the barn.

We quietly walked home in the moonlight.

Ellen's Story

CHAPTER 13

Nineteen thirty one was a long summer. No longer really than any other year, but to us it seemed that way. There was a 'hole' in our picnics and berry picking excursions. There were only three of us going to and from school. There was no more 'big brother' help with our homework lessons.

There were times I stopped at DeJongs after school to walk home with Pa when supper time came. Till then Olga and I would do our homework together at the kitchen table after having had refreshed ourselves with a glass of milk and a cookie. Sometimes Peter would help us with our arithmetic; he was good at numbers. In other subjects where some explaining would be needed, Andrew was our willing home teacher. A word of encouragement was his way of saying he had to go help with chores. He left us feeling good in ourselves.

Peter still carried my books from school. I would carry the two empty lard pail lunch buckets. It was his way of saying "I'm stronger than you so I'll take the heavier load but you can help with the lighter load." Togetherness developed between us.

There were warm summer sunny days with a light breeze blowing when Ma and I would walk the mile to DeJongs for an afternoon chat. Ma and Mrs. DeJong would hug each other and then take their lemonade and cookies to the rocking chairs in the shade of the veranda. Olga and I would take our treats to the shade of the big spruce tree in the middle of the lawn. Here we would 'share' them with our dolls. Periodically and unwillingly we'd have to share with the birds.

Winter came: Christmas school concerts, Christmas at home all done with an emptiness that was hard to ignore.

Dianne Osborne

Summer and winter came again and again. Time was healing. Although Andrew would be forever in our hearts, other events were happening that took precedence over our loss.

Pa never bought any more machinery to help make him more independent. He had a good working relationship with Mr. DeJong, and it seemed to be satisfactory to both parties. There was no big increase in livestock, only calves and foals that were born in the barn. The land was worked as it was needed, no more than that.

Laughter for Pa and giggling for Mrs. DeJong was part of their lives, but it was waning. Too many loses and too many hardships had taken the fun away. Without their jollity it put the rest of us into a slump, a slump that grew as conditions grew worse.

Many times we kids would hear the adults talk about lower grain and cattle prices. It didn't mean too much to us except maybe less money, which was not a real concern for us. But as the years passed and the dust storms came, treats were fewer and fewer. This affected us.

Pa continued to work for Mr. DeJong as long as he could. The cash flow stopped after a couple of years of dust storms. The use of Mr. DeJong's machinery became Pa's payments. He even gave Pa some grain on credit to help Pa along, but even Pa had to put a stop to that. After the pig had his delectable buttery supper, Pa knew he was beat. Like I previously said, Pa laughed no more.

Pa developed a cough he couldn't shake. With no money for a visit to the doctor to find the cause of it, he just blamed the cough on the dust. It also affected his throat, Pa complaining of it being sore. It was difficult to swallow his food so he ate less. He lost weight, weight he couldn't afford to lose.

Ma started to gain weight, not the hard solid kind in one spot, but loose and soft all over. She didn't eat anymore than us. We all shared equally as there really wasn't much in the pantry. Gardens were non-existent and livestock had to be sold for one reason or another. We still kept a few chickens for eggs. But for other staple foods like rice and flour, we had to apply for relief, receiving $2.00 a month to buy these staples and anything else.

Mr. DeJong would bring us some milk when he had extra. He would also bring us our groceries when he went to town with his tractor and wagon to get his own supplies. He didn't drive his car anymore. The gas was too expensive. Tractor gas he could still afford.

Lack of food was not the only thing we suffered from. I could no longer go to school. To me that was suffering. I enjoyed the walk with Peter and Olga. I enjoyed the lessons and the stories the teacher would read to us right after lunch. I enjoyed the fellowship of my other friends.

Olga knew of my thirst for knowledge. She knew much about me as we had always shared with each other our dreams, our sorrows, and our gossip. We became like sisters, hers being so much older than us, they were like strangers. We shared everything.

After she learned I couldn't afford to go to school, she brought her books so she could teach me that day's lesson. We missed Andrew when it came to more difficult lessons, but I was at least still learning something, including the gossip and events that were still happening at school.

On days when Mrs. DeJong needed Olga's help, Peter would come. Many times after lessons we'd take a walk (weather permitting) along the creek and talk or look for flowers or rocks or prairie cacti. We'd watch the hawks soar on the wind or swoop down to catch a wayward mouse. There was always something to see or talk about, even the shapes of the fluffy white clouds against the blue prairie open sky.

53

On the last day of lessons for the summer, we took such a walk. Just before returning, Peter found a dandelion and placed it in my braid above my ear and smiled a gentle smile, one I had never seen before.

I was very conscious of his closeness as we strolled towards the yard. So much so that it was almost uncomfortable. But how could that be? Peter and I had known each other since I was two and he was four years of age—eleven years.

As we came close to home, Peter suggested we stop in the shade of the barn to cool off. "Alright," I said. "The sun is quite warm, isn't it?"

"Yeah," was all he said.

Peter leaned against the grey weather-beaten boards of the barn, and I did the same. "Sitting would be more relaxing," I thought but I continued to stand against the boards because Peter was.

"You look different today, Ellen," Peter said breaking the silence.

"How do you mean?" I asked bewildered.

He stood in front of me and said softly, "You have bumps in your blouse."

Suddenly I felt self-conscious of my new growth. A loose blouse usually hid my coming into womanhood, but Peter had noticed. I blushed and hung my head.

Using his forefinger on my chin he lifted my head, and there was that wonderful smile again. "I'd like to see them," he said huskily.

Remembering Ma's advice about private parts, I said, "But they should be seen only by a special person."

"I'm special, aren't I?" he said as he began to undo the buttons of my blouse.

I couldn't say anything, only think, "Yes, Peter, you are special."

Ellen's Story

He opened my blouse wide and then ran his hands gently over my light brown soft nipples. I closed my eyes. I had never dreamed anything could feel so good, so heavenly. It was like I was floating.

Then ever so gently he brushed his lips against them, followed by a gentle brush on my lips. I tingled, I shook, I knew I shouldn't be letting him, but it felt so good, so right that it was Peter making me feel as if I had died and gone to heaven.

Taking the ribbons from by braids, he loosed them and combed them with his fingers. Laying the loosened waves on my breasts, covering them he whispered, "You are my own Lady Godiva."

We stood a moment longer looking at each other, not knowing exactly what to do next but not wanting to leave each other's company. Finally, with a sigh, Peter said, "I guess I'd better get home to help with chores."

My ribbons were tied at my ears causing my hair to be caught, yet free. He rebuttoned my blouse and then placed my hair over my breasts.

"You're mine now, Ellen," he said as he held me close. "Yes, Peter," was all I could say.

All these memories passed before my eyes as the clock ticked away the night. Some were good, some were bad. The last was the best of all.

I reached my hand under my nightgown and ran my own hands over my new breasts. Definitely not the same sensation. It took Peter's gentleness to make me soar to new heights. When will it happen again? How soon? How far?

As the golden dawn put out the lights of the sky, I fell asleep wondering about the future.

CHAPTER 14

The future looked bleak—weather-wise. How many more years could the prairie people take the drought? The winters were cold. Some died because they couldn't afford coal. Some areas were not so hard hit by the wind, but we lived near the ravine where the wind liked to travel.

The future looked bleak—school was out for the summer. Even though I saw Olga and Peter often, I never knew when. The daily expectations of their arrival had to be put to the back of my mind. Anxiety took the forefront. Needless to say, it was really Peter I wanted to see.

The future looked bleak—Pa's health was deteriorating. Pa wheezed rather than breathed. During the dust storms a wet cloth had to be held over his nose and mouth to allow Pa to take in air. After a storm, he would spend his time coughing and spitting, sometimes spitting up blood.

The future looked bleak—unemployment was rife. Some of it due to the weather, some due to Black Friday, and some of it due to the eminence of war between Germany and Britain.

As a young girl in her early teens, I didn't understand a great deal what was happening in the world, what was happening to us as a family, and what was happening to me.

I only knew I wanted to know more. When Mr. DeJong brought our groceries and mail—which was scarce having no utility bills and only a small note now and then from Ireland—he always brought us the newspapers of the last month. It was the daily newspaper from the city, but Mr. DeJong could afford only the weekend edition, yet that was enough. Pa and I poured over them and learned the conditions in the world of music, the world of sports, and the world in general with emphasis on the national unemployment and Churchill's pleading to the British people to take heed of Germany's and Hitler's intentions and actions.

As for us as a family, it was natural for us to become closer to each other. There were no outside chores for Pa to do. The few chickens we had fended for themselves, feeding on insects and grasshoppers. In winter, a handful of grain supplied by the DeJongs and handed out by me gave them enough sustenance to supply us with a few eggs.

Ma's weight prohibited her from doing some of the heftier household chores. I tried to do some of them; others had to be left.

On good days—weather and health-wise—Pa would want to take a stroll along the edge of the ravine. He would lean on me with one hand, the other using a willow stick he had fashioned into a cane. Whenever we passed a certain spot near the young poplar and spruce trees that were struggling to survive, Pa would stop and make the sign of the Holy Cross across his chest as he had been taught as a child in the Catholic church in his homeland of Ireland.

One day I asked him, "Why do you do that, Pa?"

"It's haloed ground, Sprig," he said. "Haloed ground."

"What do you mean, Pa?"

Tears would moisten his eyes. "Not now, Sprig," he whispered,

I knew it was useless to press him for more information.

In the evening, we would discuss the day's events, elaborating on everything, as there really wasn't much happening. It was also good exercise for our minds. Ma then would read from the Bible after which Pa would cross himself. Ma had long ago stopped admonishing Pa for doing that as she finally decided to let him have his own Catholic religion. After all, he wasn't interfering with her Protestant faith. By their mutual respect for each other's beliefs, their own relationship was much the better for it.

Dianne Osborne

Following the Bible reading, Ma would write in her journal; the sun would set and we would retire.

Even though the world and the future had an unpleasant outlook, life was bearable as long as you didn't grieve for something you couldn't have. This was my problem.

I didn't long for any of the fancy dresses or jewelry Ma and I found in the old catalogues and the odd magazine we received courtesy of the older DeJong girls who were working in the city. Pictures of fancy homes and gardens were pleasant to look at but were not coveted. What I wanted was the repeat of Peter's touch.

Peter had to take Andrew's place on the farm. The DeJongs were well established by the time we took up our homestead. Therefore there was a great deal of maintenance and caring for animals to be done. Their house was large and fully furnished, needing its own special care. Olga helped her Mother in this area and also helped in the baking and in the garden that had home grown fertilizer to help it along. Water was hauled from their well. Being a healthy family also helped their situation.

But it didn't help mine. The memory of Peter's touch caused some sleepless nights making me irritable from time to time. Pa noticed my mood swings. I overheard him asking Ma what was the matter with me.

"Well, Kelly, Ellen is growing up. She has started her cycles. You know how cranky I get at those times."

"Yes, I sure do," Pa emphasized his agreement.

"Well, our little girl has begun her womanhood." Ma left it at that.

I was glad for Ma's explanation. I let them think that was the reason for my unpredictable moods.

The odd time, the DeJongs would come for a Sunday afternoon chat. We three teenagers would wander off on our own. Olga would gossip and Peter would tell her not to, but he never left our company. When he could he would touch my fingers or arm. Sometimes he would discreetly look directly at the front of my blouse and then wink. The thrill that would soar through me was able to keep my spirits up for a few days after their visit.

Life went on. Olga spent one more winter at school while Peter stayed home. The next year she was too old for the one room schoolhouse. This ended my lessons as well.

In 1937, we both turned fourteen years old, too old for dolls and coloring books, and as far as our parents were concerned too young for boys.

"But not too young to go to work," said Olga on one of her rare visits. "Mother and Father feel I need some outside experience so they have spoken to Mr. Black at the general store. I start Monday, cleaning shelves, keeping things tidy, and waiting on the customers. Eventually, I'll be able to ring the items on the till. I'm a little excited, but it just seems that we have so little time as it is to be together, and now there will be even less time. Oh, well, I guess that is all part of growing up," she added wistfully.

I knew she was unhappy as not one giggle had escaped her throat.

Her unhappiness rubbed off on me. Without her, Peter's visits would be very rare as he only came when she came. He was sixteen now, almost a young man and in great demand by his father.

Listlessness and boredom began to creep in. I mentioned my feelings and Olga's employment to Ma and Pa on one of our evening discussions. They were quiet for a moment or two.

Then Pa, always the entrepreneur of the family, voiced an idea.

"Since Olga is no longer at home on Mondays, why don't you go see Zelda, I mean Mrs. DeJong, and offer to help her on washing day? Whether or not they can pay you anything doesn't matter. You will have something to look forward to, a sort of purpose in your life."

"But Ma needs me on washing day," I argued.

"I'm sure Ma can change her day to Tuesday. We have so few things to wash. There is so little else happening here; I can't see that the day Ma does her washing will make that much difference to the world or, for that matter, to us. What do you say, Ma?"

Ma looked at Pa, and Pa looked at Ma. He knew she would agree. Rarely had she contradicted his wishes except when he wanted to do some horse dealing. It remained a mystery to me for some years as to why she disliked him doing something that would bring more horses or money into the household.

"Whatever you say, Kelly," she meekly sighed.

"There, that's all settled then. Monday morning, Sprig, you put a clean dress on and make your way down to the DeJongs and make an offer of your services to the lady of the house. Ha. Ha. I haven't felt this good in a long time."

A cough suppressed a chuckle gurgling in his throat. Then another and another till soon Pa was sweating with the excursion. Ma ran for a glass of water, and I tried to comfort him as best I could. Finally, he was able to lie down on the lumpy couch and rest, breathing heavily.

Monday morning came, and in a way it came all too soon. As I walked the mile to our neighbours, I felt a little shaky and nervous. "What is the matter with you, Ellen?" I scolded myself. "You have been at the DeJongs many, many times. They are definitely not strangers." "But this was to ask for work," the other half of my mind argued. "This is a totally different situation. She might say no." Pa would be so disappointed if she did. His gentle hug this morning as I left told me he was counting on me.

Ellen's Story

So I continued on down the road and onto DeJong's lane. I was just about ready to knock when Mr. DeJong and Peter came out the door.

"Well, good morning, Ellen. What brings you here so early?" His greeting was cheery but then turned to concern. "Your Ma and Pa are not sick, are they?"

"No, they are not, thank you. Good morning to you too, Mr. DeJong. I–I, well, I'd like to talk to Mrs. DeJong if I may?"

"You certainly may, young lady." He opened the door and called "Zelda. Ellen is here. She would like to chat with you. See you later, Ellen." He closed the door behind me as I entered into their bright kitchen.

"Why, Ellen, it is so nice to see you," said Mrs. DeJong, giving me a hug and kiss on the cheek. She was cheerful as usual, but the giggle was rarely heard now. Andrew had taken that with him.

"Thank you, Mrs. DeJong. And it is nice to see you, too." Then I hesitated.

Realizing I wanted to say something and having not heard my conversation with Mr. DeJong, she, too, voiced her concern over Ma and Pa's health.

"No, no, they are fine. Yes, they are fine. I just came–well, I was wondering…"

I bit my lip, and she kindly encouraged me to go on. "Yes, Ellen, what were you wondering?"

"Well…" I said slowly, and then blurted out everything. "I was just wondering if you could use some help on wash days now that Olga has a full time job in town. I thought maybe just on wash days because that is such a big chore, and Ma doesn't mind changing her wash day to Tuesday so I can come help you. That is if you need help. You needn't pay me. Pa wants me to know what it's like to work for someone else, and we thought maybe you might need some help on washdays. And so I came to ask if you needed me."

There, it was out. Mrs. DeJong stood with an astonished look on her face then stammered, "Well, I don't know. I just don't know." (My heart fell.) "But goodness I do think it's a good idea. There is so much to do on wash days." Getting a firm hold on herself she added "Yes, Ellen, you shall work for me on wash days. You can start by clearing off the table while I pull the washing machine out to the sink. Then we'll go from there."

I let out a sigh of relief and hugged her.

Mrs. DeJong chattered all morning, so different from Ma's silent 'conversations'. Around 10 o'clock, Mr. DeJong came in to take a couple of cups of coffee and some cookies out to the back door step for Peter and himself. After ten or fifteen minutes, they were gone again.

Noontime brought Mr. DeJong and Peter in to the porch where they washed in a basin and then throwing the dirty water out the door where some grass was trying to grow. Their yard was greener than ours having been there longer, but still there were patches of drying grass especially near the house where the sun beat so hot.

We lunched on fresh biscuits, soup, cookies and wild berries preserved in a jar. Maybe to them it was a meager meal; to me it was a feast.

I tried to eat as much as I could so as not to insult Mrs. DeJong's cooking, but Peter sat right across the table from me. I knew he wasn't always looking at me, but his presence and my memories made me nervous. I concentrated fully on trying to eat.

Mr. DeJong noticed my silence and said, "Ellen, you're awfully quiet. Ah. I know. This is the first time here as an employee. Well, we're not any different than when you come as a neighbour. We enjoy your company. Don't let a little work get in the way of our friendship."

"Yes, sir. Thank you, sir," I quietly mumbled.

That wasn't the reason for my silence, but if he wanted to think that way, I wasn't going to change his thoughts. Peter and I exchanged a quick glance. I think he knew.

The rest of the day went well. Just before supper, Mr. DeJong fired up the tractor and headed to town to pick up Olga. Peter volunteered to walk me home. "I'll carry the quart sealer of milk for you," he said.

It was good to walk just with Peter with no one else around. The late afternoon sun was still warm, and we both had put in a good day's work so we didn't hurry. Even our talk was slow.

We reached the end of our treeless lane, and in so doing we also reached the end of the road that led past DeJongs and on into town. A big pile of dirt blocked the motorists' way because of the ravine. There were no settlers on the other side of the ravine needing no bridge across it. The depression helped the municipality counselors decide against building something that was not necessary.

This dirt monument had been a great playground for "King of the Castle" summer and winter, using it to full capacity with the other friends from school, especially on birthdays.

So it was natural for us to find a lump of dirt that could be used as a temporary chair, and there we sat quietly.

"How did you enjoy your day?" Peter asked.

"It was a good day, Peter," I answered.

"How often are you going to be there?" he wanted to know.

"Every wash day. That will make it every Monday," I replied.

"I'm glad we'll be able to see each other more often."

"I'm glad, too, Peter."

Dianne Osborne

Peter put his arm around my shoulders then gave me a little kiss on the lips.

"I better get back," he said huskily. "Father and Olga will soon be home, and Mother will have supper on the table." He helped me to my feet and handed me the jar of milk. I watched him disappear down the road before going up to the house.

Ma had biscuits and beans and had made a small cake in celebration of my first day of work.

"We can each have a small glass of milk to wash everything down," I said as I produced the jar of fresh milk.

"Well, now." Pa beamed. "That's not too bad for pay. A quart of milk in town is 10¢ and a lunch is about 15¢ so you have made your 25¢ a day that most cleaning ladies get. Well done, Sprig." He pulled my hair that I wore tied at my ears and falling loose just as Peter had showed me two long years ago.

I anticipated a visit from Olga that evening but to no avail. She didn't come the next evening or the next. I was beginning to think that she was annoyed that someone, especially me, would try to take her place at home. With time on your hands you think of all kinds of stupid things. On Thursday evening, she knocked on our screen door and then came bursting into our house calling my name.

"Ellen, Ellen," she cried. When I came from the living room, she threw her arms around me and exclaimed, "I'm so glad Mother has you to help her on washdays. I don't have to feel guilty any more about leaving Mother with all the washing to do. Thank you, thank you, thank you." And she hugged me again.

I should have known she would be glad for me. The whole family would rejoice for other people's happiness yet would be full of concern and willingness to help when you were down.

"Come, Ellen," she urged. "Let's go for a walk. But first I have to say 'hello' to your Ma and Pa."

Ellen's Story

Having said her greetings, we went out to walk along the edge of the ravine. We found our cluster of rocks that were placed conveniently for a tête-à-tête. We used them for that purpose.

Olga was still her bubbly and giggly self. She was young enough that Andrew's death wasn't capable of depriving her of that part of her personality. So we–she–talked.

"Do you remember Tom from school? He was a grade ahead of us."

"Yes, I think so," I answered, wondering what she was leading up to. "Wasn't he kind of chubby with a round face?"

"Yes, that's him. Oh, Ellen, I'm so glad you remember him." She gave my arm a squeeze. "Well, he came into the store about a week ago and saw me working there and seemed glad to see me. Well, one thing led to another and guess what?" she exclaimed excitedly.

"Oh, Olga, I can't guess," I said fully knowing she didn't want me to guess as she wanted to tell the whole story.

"He's working at the elevator, and now that he knows I'm in town too, he brings his lunch to the store and we eat our lunches together on the bench outside the store. I don't know, but I think I have a boyfriend. but don't tell Mother. I'll do that when I'm sure. Promise?"

"Of course, Olga. I'm so glad for you. I guess it would be nice to have a boyfriend," I added lamely.

"Ellen, of all people to say that especially since you've had Peter all these years."

I felt my face grow warm. Did our love for each other really show? We try so hard to keep it to ourselves. I continued to ponder about this while Olga continued to talk about Tom, town, her job, etc., etc., until the sun told us we should be parting. With a hug and kiss she left for home in a flurry.

CHAPTER 15

Rain was beginning to fall more frequently that summer. I was fourteen but not enough to make a difference in the agriculture world. Dust storms still occurred but not in their previous furious manner. The quietness and stillness in the air–the calm before the storm–still gave you a warning to batten down the hatches in preparation for whatever–light or heavy onslaught of wind and dirt.

I often wondered if Ma and Pa were conscious of the weather. Did a cloudy day make them feel gloomy or did it give them a sort of comfort, peace, and security as if the clouds were a blanket protecting them from the hot sun, from the deprivations of their own lives, from the turbulence and the stress of the outside world?

Did a sunny day give them buoyancy or did the hot sun beat down on them suffocating, suppressing, and causing depression?

They seemed, to me, to be quite content in just being together, being thankful for each day that came along. Ma would attend to her daily household tasks that didn't take long to do being that there wasn't much to attend to. A meager breakfast, lunch, and supper, dishes washed once a day to conserve water, sweep the floors, make the beds, and one day a week to wash our few bits of clothing and linens.

Pa still rose early in the morning to slowly make his rounds of the yard stopping for only a moment at the 'holy spot' by the spindly trees. When it rained, he spent his time in the barn doing what we didn't know. This was his quiet time. By the time breakfast was over, he was ready for a nap on the couch.

As for me, after my few small chores, I'd walk along the creek to check out which prairie flower had bloomed over night, to watch a mama sparrow feed her young, to watch the wild grass that took over the cropland to wave in the wind conjuring up visions of what the sea must have looked like as we crossed over.

Rainy days found me in my bedroom, listless, thinking how much more fun a rainy day was as a child when I could dress and undress my only doll and cut out pretty ladies and dresses from the catalogue to have them parade across my bedroom floor. Now, I resorted to rereading the magazines from the older DeJong girls and dream of the day when maybe, just maybe, I could have long red fingernails. I envied their full lips in bright red lipstick and hair piled high on their heads.

With Olga in town everyday and Peter helping his father every day, my days were long. Sewing and needlework was out of the question; there wasn't any material to work with. Besides, when something was made what use would it be. Ma's table linens continued to lay idle in her buffet drawer.

We didn't go anywhere needing new or remodeled clothing. Even if there was money, Ma wasn't interested in organizations or clubs. Pa was her world. Pa, on the other hand, although not wanting to get involved in anything organized, did enjoy people. His inability to walk to town, I think, was a bit of a sore spot for him. When we gathered in the living room, mostly in the evening, Pa would reminisce about our first few years when he was so full of life and expectations. As always, when he talked of horses, his eyes would get a faraway look and he'd forget he had an audience. His mind no longer controlled his voice box and silence would tell us he was off on his horse or horse dealing.

We didn't go to church, partly due to the difference in Ma and Pa's religion. Pa would allow Ma to read from the Bible, and every now and then, when he would agree to something, he would make the sign of the cross across his chest.

And so we existed in our humdrum life.

On the following Sunday, after Olga's evening visit, Olga and Peter delighted us once again with their presence. I noticed them walking up the road and felt good. I was getting company. But I also knew I would share this company. I wanted so much for Ma and Pa to be happy. I realized maybe they were happy; they had each other and although I knew they loved me very much, I was still alone. I had no personal partner. It sometimes it felt like I was the odd spoke in the wheel.

Sitting at the lunch table at DeJongs made me feel wanted. There were four of us, two couples, and now that I was becoming familiar with Mondays, it was usually a cheerful lunch hour.

As I watched, I could see that Olga was her cheerful talkative self, and I could hear faintly the tinkle of her giggle. I could see, also, that she was becoming quite an attractive girl, filling out in all the right places, becoming slim—not skinny, not plump. Peter's physique was still skinny even though he should have been developing more, being that he was two years older than us. Maybe it was stress that kept him that way. He was conscientious about everything and disturbingly conscious of a wayward lock of long blond hair that continually irritated him by refusing to stay in place when pushed back. Many was the time, I noticed as they came, his left hand reaching up to push that radical piece of hair back off of his face. When they arrived at our place of residence it was hanging in his eyes.

On this afternoon, Ma and Pa were sitting on the bench on the south side of the old shed we had called home on first coming here. There was a bit of a northern breeze cooling the August sun but on the bench all was warm and sheltered. I was sitting on the grass at their feet while Ma read the scriptures.

Olga was apologetic when she realized they had come at a time when family devotions were being held. We all assured her it was a pleasure to see them and to please stay.

Ellen's Story

"Oh, I'm so glad to have friends such as yourselves," Olga exclaimed. "Peter has come just to visit but, I, Ellen," and she grabbed me by the shoulders since I was standing by this time, "have such good news for you. I'm so excited I can hardly tell it."

I didn't say anything as I knew she didn't need prompting.

She began. "The day before yesterday, elderly Mrs. Walker came in to the store. She is such a dear soul, so pleasant, so neat in her dress, and I daresay there is not a hair out of place under her hat. Anyways, she came into the store. She comes in almost every day to buy something for her supper. She's English and still had a slight accent. It's such a pleasure to listen to her talk. And quite frequently talk is what she and I do. She's become such a dear friend to me. Of course, not as much as you are, dear Ellen, but you know what I mean.

Anyway we fell to talking. She said that I was such a sweet young girl to help such an elderly lady–and of course, I thanked her for the compliment–and she wondered if I knew any other sweet young lady who would be willing to help her clean her house. Well, needless to say, I immediately thought of you, dear Ellen. I said I did know someone, but I'd like to talk to her first.

"Oh, of course." Mrs. Walker said. "I need her to wash my floors, dust, and just do a weekly clean up. I do so like to have my house clean for Sunday. Sometimes my family comes from the city to visit, and I don't want them to think I'm incapable of looking after myself." And she gives me a wink. Isn't she a dear?"

"And so Ellen, what do you say? You can help Mother on Mondays and you can help Mrs. Walker on Saturdays. She said she'd be willing to pay the going rate of 25¢ per day."

I stuttered. "I–I don't know. I'd have to get up really early to walk in. I'd really like to do it if Ma and Pa say it's okay. It's just the matter on how to get there and still be able to do a good job."

"Oh," exclaimed Olga, "that's not too great of a problem. Mrs. Walker likes to sleep in at least until 7:30 so you wouldn't have to be there until 9 a.m. That's when I start work. I took the liberty of asking Father if you could ride with us so you would only have to walk to our place and that's only a mile. I've taken care of that for you," she added with a gleam of satisfaction.

"Olga, you are so kind." I gave her a huge hug and then turned to Ma and Pa.

"Would it be alright with you? Can you spare me another day?"

Pa's eyes were watery when he said, "Of course, we can. It's wonderful news you bring to us, Olga. And I thank you from all of us."

"Yes, Olga," I said. "And I thank you most of all."

We chatted a spell longer while Peter remained silent. We all understood that when Olga gets wound up, nobody has a chance to say anything. Soon she was exclaiming, "Oh, Peter. We'd best get going. Come along, Peter. Bye for now. See you later." They made their way down the lane waving cheerily.

Pa chuckled after they had left. Such a pleasant sound it was. Olga had brought it out. Pa said, "You would think Olga was the elder of the two the way she bosses Peter about. But Peter doesn't seem to mind. Much like his father he is. He'll make a good solid husband to some lucky girl." Pa looked straight at me.

I knew I had to get some sleep that night as washday was a heavy day, but the afternoon kept flooding back. I was excited about this new job. Olga was going to let Mrs. Walker know that I would be willing to work for her and then Olga was to let me know when I was to start. But what kept coming back to my mind's eye more than the prospect of another job was Peter's wink and special smile as he said his farewells. I was in heaven. Who cared whether or not the sun shone.

Ellen's Story

During the week, Olga came bubbling into our yard to say I could start this Saturday morning. Confirmation was made that I could ride in with her and her father who would take me up to Mrs. Walkers to introduce me to her. She was so excited you would think she had the job, not I. That was Olga.

When I arrived home in the early evening from my first day at Mrs. Walker's, I found the kitchen table—the only one we had—all dressed in Irish linen and English china.

"Oh, Ma," I exclaimed, " that looks beautiful."

"Thank you, Ellen. Pa and I felt we should have another little celebration but a better one since you are making real money on this job. Our best daughter deserves the best. We're very proud of you and are so happy for you."

I put my arms around Ma and tried to give her ample body a tight squeeze. "Thank you, Ma and you too, Pa."

Frankfurters and beans had never tasted so good. There was even a small white icing-less cake, not as fluffy as it should have been as Ma probably had to skimp on the eggs. To me it tasted delicious; it tasted like their love for me.

After the elegance of the supper table was replaced in their drawers and cupboards, Ma brought her rocking chair into the living room, and Pa laid down on the couch. They patiently waited while I took my habitual place at the window—my window to the world as it became in the future. I knew they wanted to hear about my day.

They seemed to hang on to my every word as I told them about the pump in the kitchen sink that was connected to a cistern beneath the house. A pipe connected to the eave troughs that caught the rain from the roof filled the cistern. Mrs. Walker never had to draw water from a well.

I told them about the narrow strips of red-brown wood that made up the living and dining room floors. My job was to wash, wax,

Dianne Osborne

and polish those floors till they shone. I also had to polish the round pedestal dining table and then replace the lace tablecloth and center-piece of a crystal bowl filled with fresh flowers Mrs. Walker had picked from her flower garden.

Exchanging the doilies on the sofa and chair and exchanging the needlepoint cushion covers for clean ones was another pleasant job. All the while during part of the afternoon, rainbows danced on the walls covered in rose-design wallpaper. They danced on the white-fringed shade of the floor lamp that needed only a push of a button for it to light. They danced on the polished floor and scatter rugs. They came from the prisms hanging in the lace-curtained windows.

A striking grandfather clock that kept company with her ances-tral portraits hanging on the wall chimed the hour, competing with the cuckoo clock in the kitchen.

"All her furniture was of the finest wood like you see in the pic-tures of the magazines. Her china was thin and housed in glass-doored cupboards. When we had lunch we used plain but pleasant kitchen dishes. She made tea in a brown-betty pot and served sand-wiches with store bought bread. Dessert was her homemade cookies. Ma, it was like being in paradise. Even her yard was neat with green grass and some flowers. There was…"

I stopped talking. They weren't listening anymore. Ma had a misty faraway look in her eyes. Pa noticed it, patted her hand, and then turned over to show his back to us. Ma sighed then heaved her-self out of her chair, retrieved her Bible and journal from the buffet drawer, returning to her chair.

I went up to my room. The day had been so full of various kinds of emotions: nervousness at meeting Mrs. Walker, relief at her pleas-antness, pride in myself on how well I was able to please her, excite-ment at getting my first full 25¢ pay, and pleasure at seeing Ma and Pa's excitement over my good fortune. Suddenly, all those joyous

72

feelings came crashing down around my head and shoulders. I threw myself down on my bed and cried.

"You're just tired," I told myself. "Don't blame yourself for making Ma and Pa feel guilty about not providing the same kind of home. Circumstances were different."

CHAPTER 16

S oon after I had started at Mrs. Walker's, a Mrs. Switzer from down the street required my services. This was wonderful news. Ma and Pa agreed. I would now be making 50¢ a week, which came to $2.00 a month, as much as we were getting on relief. I could buy food other than beans, and I could buy coal to keep us warm next winter.

Eagerly, I went to Mrs. Switzer's. In anticipation, I looked forward to cleaning another nice house and working in a pleasant atmosphere.

My bubble burst when I stepped into Mrs. Switzer's shabby but somewhat clean house. Her greeting was curt, putting me immediately to work. Work was what I came for so I did not complain. However, my new employer was not a pleasant one. While washing her dishes—they must have been left for a numbers of days; quantity and dried on food told me that—she hovered over me like a hawk, examining the silverware and glasses for streaks. Washing the bare wooded floors was no easy task, especially when the lady of the house stood watching in the doorway, calling out all the spots I had missed. Many of them I knew I had missed and was preparing to do them. I kept telling myself, "She can't read my mind."

Eventually, that first day was over. I was tired and troubled as I climbed into the wagon beside Olga. As her father drove the tractor, Olga and I shared our day. Her cheerfulness buoyed me up enabling me to put on a good front once I got home. I didn't want Ma and Pa to be unhappy.

The next two Thursdays weren't any better. The Thursday that became the last one was the worst of all.

The dishes must have been left in the warming oven of the cooking range or in the sun. The food was so dried on it took me ages to get it off. Hot water seemed to be the most help so I placed the dishpan on the cooking range to keep the water hot. The range had to have a fire going in it to heat water for washing the windows, floors, etc. The heat, the steam, and the sun's hot rays coming through closed windows soon made the small kitchen close and stuffy. All this did not put me in a very good frame of mind.

After dishes came the washing of the kitchen windows that should have been done first as the sun was not shining on those panes when I arrived. But you don't contradict your elders especially when they are your employer. So with a great deal of difficulty and time I was able to wash the windows streak free.

A meager lunch of a piece of bread and cheese washed down with weak tea prepared me for the afternoon of scrubbing with hot water, lye soap, and scrub brush on the living room floor of unpainted wood boards.

First, I swept the floor with a corn broom moving the sofa and chair to get the dust from underneath. Washing was started in the far corner backing myself to the doorway leading to the kitchen at which spot Mrs. Switzer sat on a wooden straight-backed chair. As I proceeded, the sofa and chair had to be moved again to wash where they stood. After replacing them in the exact spot and at the right angle, the instructor made sure I cleaned up my footprints on the wet part of the floor.

I continued scrubbing, knowing her eyes were on my every movement. She didn't say anything only when ordering a job done. I didn't mind that she didn't make conversation; I needed all my brainpower to concentrate on trying to please her.

I came to the doorway, finishing the last spot. I moved from my hands and knees position to sit on my haunches while I squeezed the rag free of water. At that moment—how it was actually done, I don't know, but I have my suspicions–the pail of water tipped over spewing all the dirty water back onto the freshly washed living room floor.

Mrs. Switzer screamed, "Now look what you have done, you clumsy girl. I can't understand how Mrs. Walker can be so happy with your work. You're slow and you're clumsy. Now hurry up and mop this water up."

Fortunately for me, the living room floor had a sag in the middle, and that is where much of the water stayed. Through tears, I mopped and squeezed as fast as I could. When finished, I threw the water, pail, and all out into the backyard and ran down the street past Mrs. Walker's, down near the elevators, and on out on to the road leading home.

It was only then did I slow to a fast walk. My heart beat painfully inside my chest, my breath came in great gulps, and sweat ran down my face and neck. I didn't know what time it was; I didn't care. Maybe I would care by the time I walked the five miles, but at the moment, I was too frustrated to care about anything.

I walked fast and then ran a little and then back to a fast walk. I had to get away from that horrible woman as fast as I could. I thought of her unfriendly nature, of her stinginess–on one of my paydays she gave me a dime, two nickels, and four pennies saying she just couldn't find another penny. In my young mind, I was able to sympathize with Pa when he was short-changed by a farmer Pa had helped with harvest. Little did I know until later the real reason for Pa bringing home less than what he should have.

Now I began to worry about Ma and Pa. Unless I found another house to clean my monthly wage is now back down to $1.00. We would still be able to buy coal; I'd make sure of that. Pa was so skinny he needed lots of heat to keep warm.

Ellen's Story

But what are they going to say when I tell them how rude I was by not putting away the mop pail and other things, and that I didn't apologize for knocking over the pail in the first place.

The more I thought of the incident, the more I began to believe she deliberately kicked the pail over herself. Why? I didn't know. Thinking back, I recalled a slight movement of her foot as my hands entered the pail to rinse the rag.

Ma and Pa had respect for their elders, and they taught me to have the same respect. They would want me to apologize whether it was my fault or not. My Irish was up and stamping my foot extra hard as I hurried on my way, I said out loud and in a determined voice, "I will NOT apologize to ol' lady Switzer."

Such was my frustration that I hadn't noticed that the light breeze of the day had stopped. I was having difficulty breathing but that was from running and walking fast. Right? Wrong.

Just as I recognized the lull before the storm, the dirt of the road began to swirl around me. The roar of the wind enveloped me and tore at my clothes. Reality told me that I was in the middle of nowhere–how far away from shelter I did not know–with only my apron that I was lifting to my face to protect me.

The combination of the apron and dirt in my face took away my vision. I still continued on, stumbling, not sure of my direction or even if I was still on the road. My toe caught on something; I made a few quick steps as in an Irish jig to try to keep my balance. It was a fruitless attempt. I fell hitting my head. The darkness of the storm deepened. I lay still and quiet, my face buried in my apron.

CHAPTER 17

It's been two years since I woke up on the side of the road covered with fine dirt and dead grasses. I'm not sure whether it was the quiet that woke me or the way the brain works to awaken the senses when danger is near. I struggled to sit, digging myself out, awkwardly fumbling as my head pounded with pain. I was not having a successful time orientating myself. In every direction were fields of dead grass or ripening grain, blue skies and space all pictured with fuzzy edges. The only thing I was sure of was that I was alone and far from home.

I tried to stand and then to take a step. The flat prairie plate tipped and I reached for the ground, deciding that sitting would be a better idea. I couldn't, however, sit here forever. Somewhere, far off in the back of my mind I knew I had a mother and a father. Where were they? Another man and woman—no, it was a young girl—came into focus. Where were they? It seemed I should be with them. Why wasn't I?

"Settle down, Ellen," I told myself. Realistically, I didn't want to do anything anyway. My head hurt; my brain was not functioning right. The sun was warm, the breeze gentle, soothing me. I started to get sleepy. A number of times I was jerked awake by the sensation of toppling over sideways.

Then in the distance, I heard a familiar sound and as it became louder, the vision of a familiar object came closer. I heard above everything, an excited familiar voice. "There she is, Father. There she is. There's Ellen."

Relief, gladness, weariness, and even apprehension as to what now came flooding through me as strong yet gentle hands helped me into the wagon. When they discovered I couldn't answer their questions, I heard Olga's confident voice. "Mother will know what to do."

An hour later, I found myself wrapped in a blanket sitting in Ma's rocking chair listening to the instructions being given to Ma from Mrs. DeJong.

"She has had a slight concussion. Don't let her sleep any length of time. Even though the night is warm, she'll be thankful for the blanket. I know it is an inconvenience, but she will need to be checked hourly during the night, especially her pupils in her eyes. That goose egg on her forehead will need a cold compress."

Mrs. DeJong stepped over to me and asked, "Can you see me, Ellen?"

"Yes, I can see you. You are not as fuzzy as you were before."

"That is a blessing. So, Caroline, you can see she is already on the mend. But if things do get worse be sure to get word to me somehow. I'll send Peter over in the morning, too. Horace will let Mrs. Walker know of this. Ellen won't be able to work on Saturday."

Ma and Pa thanked the DeJongs profusely as they took their leave. I didn't hear everything except the repeat of Mrs. DeJong confirming that she would send Peter over in the morning.

A whole lot of nothing happened in those two years since the Switzer episode, and yet there was a whole lot of something occurring. That summer waned into fall followed by a real cold snowy winter. Proudly I handed over a number of my twenty-five cent pieces to Mr. DeJong when I had asked him to bring us a wagon load of coal.

Many were the days that I didn't work for Mrs. DeJong or Mrs. Walker. Likewise, many were the days Olga didn't work at the store and Tom didn't work at the elevator. The inclement weather prevented it.

Dianne Osborne

Spring came but not hot like in previous years. Farmers in all directions from our little town eagerly ploughed and seeded fields that had produced very little in the past few years. I guess they felt it in their bones, in their very heart and soul that the tide of agricultural events was going to turn.

This scenario kept Tom exceptionally busy at the elevator causing Olga to complain, "Our lunch hours are only fifteen minutes long."

"Be thankful he has a job, Olga," her father reprimanded her. "And, I hope both you girls are thankful for your jobs as well, no matter how little they pay. According to the newspapers, unemployment in the cities and various places across the country is rising. The dust storms of the past five to six years played havoc not only with farmers but big businesses as well. Even though there are jobs to do, there is no money to pay workers for their labour. If this year's crop gives us a good yield–and it looks good so far–there will be work for people around here but not for anyone else who comes in."

Many times the three of us conversed on world and local problems as we rode home on the buggy seat, Olga on one side of her father and I on the other. The two horses would trot briskly, their bells and harnesses providing background music for our thoughts and opinions. On rainy days, there was no time for this amiable companionship. Mr. DeJong came for Olga and me with the tractor. The noise of the motor kept us quiet. Besides, we needed all our wits about us as we stood on the tractor floor and hung on for dear life to the fenders covering the big back tires.

One cold miserable day, we had to stop at the railroad crossing to allow a freight train to go through. It went slowly through the town limits after which it would pick up speed. We were glad of the little bit of heat coming from the tractor's motor. It warmed our legs and feet. The rest of our bodies were battered about by the wind that was also whipping up grey and black heavy clouds. Even as a teenager I could read the clouds. Today, they said that before long rain would fall and maybe a skiff of snow, such was the coolness of the air.

I tied my kerchief on my head a little tighter, pulled up my coat collar, and put my hands in my pockets, hunching my shoulders against the autumn chill. We watched silently as the boxcars trundled past. Some had wheat in them, but most were empty, that is to say, empty of grain. The open doors framed at least a dozen or more dirty, gaunt faces of every nationality. The pathetic picture they portrayed magnified the truth of what Mr. DeJong had told Olga and me not too long ago.

The noise of the tractor prevented us from talking, but each knew the others sobering thoughts.

Ma had cooked potatoes and vegetables from the garden she finally was able to grow again. For desert there was bread and milk sprinkled with brown sugar. Pa noticed I picked at my food more than I usually did.

"Something bothering you, Sprig?" Pa asked. "Get it off of your chest before going to bed," he encouraged.

Slowly, I told Pa and Ma about the men in the boxcars. "They looked so sad. Their mouths drooped as much as their shoulders. And their eyes, Pa, they were so–so–depressing. I guess that's the best explanation. They gave me a chill colder than the wind was giving me. And, Pa, they looked so dirty."

"Probably were, Sprig," Pa said slowly and sadly. "My guess is that they hadn't had even a wash in weeks, maybe months."

I shivered at that information. Even when water was in short supply, Ma, Pa, and I still had a wash before going to bed. I would wash my hands and face first, and then Ma and then Pa would wash.

Dianne Osborne

After that I would put the basin on the floor and rinse my feet, followed by Ma, then Pa who threw the water onto the straggling raspberry bush.

It was all so confusing. I wanted to know more but wasn't sure what to ask. I stumbled, "What are they doing? Where are they going? Why are they in those boxcars?"

"Well…" Pa slowly and thoughtfully answered. "My best guess would be unemployment. You have just witnessed what I've been reading about in the papers. The destitution brought on by the drought has come to a head. There is no work at home so they are out searching. What many will find is a uniform that will send them overseas to fight the war that is speculated. Hitler's forces are becoming a menace in Europe. Churchill has been trying to warn the British for years of Hitler's schemes but they haven't been listening. It's only been recently that their eyes have opened. War is not nice, but it's better than starving. The army will give them three square meals a day and enough pay to send some back home to their families. It's the lesser of two evils, I guess."

I, too, had read about these impending prospects of war in Europe and of the declarations that Canada would be there when needed. There were advertisements encouraging 'the adventurous' to join the forces. 'Join the navy and see the world' was one enticement.

Our conversation was coinciding with the one Olga and I had had with her father. Probably every home had one of these sessions.

I continued to question Pa. "What about people with homes and jobs? Will they be asked to go to war?"

"That's called conscription, Sprig, and as yet not enforced. Anyone joining up, homeless or not, will be doing it voluntarily," Pa explained.

Of course, my mind went immediately to Peter. *Was he old enough to go? Would he volunteer?*

82

Ellen's Story

Pa interrupted my thoughts. "They say they may discourage farmers to go. The government needs food for their armies but if the farmer, young or old, is willing and eager to go and has someone capable enough to care for his farm, they'll probably accept him. Peter could go; he's just turned eighteen. But poor Tom, with his bad eyesight, they would reject him even though the rest of him is healthy."

Pa stopped to smile then added, "Tom's eyesight is so bad he couldn't see the broadside of a barn, never mind hit it with a bullet from a rifle." A little chuckle escaped his dry throat that seemed to be getting worse.

CHAPTER 18

The four of us sat around a table in the only café in town. We had just come from the theatre where we had watched a Tom Mix western movie on the big screen. We sipped our Cokes and discussed the newsreel that was shown before the movie. We were not the only ones hashing over the news. We were not the only ones who felt the atmosphere of impending doom. We were not the only ones who felt that war was close at hand.

Three weeks later, September 3, 1939, war in Europe was declared. Every day the railway boxcars carried the homeless and the others who had left their homes, carried them to the east to train in the theaters of war.

Peter usually came for a visit mid-afternoon on Sundays. Sometimes Olga would come. This particular Sunday—a day of blue skies, warm breezes, a day defying fall and winter to come—he came alone. He was very quiet and sober as he suggested, "Let's walk down the banks of the ravine to where we three built our cave."

He held my hand as we walked keeping me close to his side.

As we left the immediate yard, I said, "It's odd you should want to go to the cave. I went there not too long ago to see what had happened to it through the dust storms. I found the old metal box we used to store that old horse blanket in. The candles and matches were still there too. There is a tin cup missing. It must have been blown away, but everything else is still there."

Peter let go my hand to put his arm around my shoulder. It was just an automatic gesture that I put my arm around his waist. He said, "Well, we'll just have to make use of what is there." His face seemed to brighten.

Again he fell silent almost to the point of being uncomfortable. Very conscious of his leg touching mine, I recalled a former day of uncomfortable silence. That day turned out wonderful. Would this day be the same?

We came to the cave and examined it together. We shook out five years of dust from the blanket then laid it on the floor. Peter invited me to sit beside him then took the two tin cups handing one to me. He raised his in the air exclaiming, "To us." This was followed by pretense of drinking from the cup. I followed his example at which we both laughed.

We talked amiably for a while. Contentment began to steal through me and I think through Peter as well. A break in our conversation brought on the awkward silence again.

Unashamed, Peter turned to me and kissed me on the nose. His arm went around me pulling me to the blanket. He covered my face and neck with kisses while caressing my whole body. My blouse was removed, something that frequently happened when we were alone. Soon we were lying naked, touching skin to skin. I explored as much of him as he did of me. Emotions ran higher once I felt his manhood hot against my tummy.

Peter was always gentle with me no matter what we were doing. He was no different as we changed from children to lovers.

Afterwards we went skinny dipping in the shallow creek that ran through the ravine. Since the water came only to our knees, we had to sit on the rocks that formed the creek bed to cool our burning bodies. The sun was warm as we dried out on the grassy banks.

Noticing his arm, which lay across my stomach, was getting heavy, I looked at Peter to find he had fallen asleep. I lay still so as not to disturb him. My mind, however, worked overtime. "This is the beginning of forever," I thought. "The day has been beautiful weatherize, Peter's friendship, Peter's love, Peter's contentment, just everything had the makings of a beautiful beginning of a life together."

I was sure we would be together for forever and ever and a day. Nothing could part us now.

Waking with a start, Peter commented, "It's getting cool. Maybe we should get our clothes on." I agreed.

As we helped each other dress, Peter became pensive again. He took my hands in his looking straight into my face and said, "Ellen, this has been the most wonderful day of my life. I planned it to be and you were so wonderful at co-operating. I only wish it could continue."

Tearfully I asked, "Why can't it?"

Wetting his lips with a dry tongue he blurted out, "Because I'm taking the train to the city tomorrow morning to join the army. Then I'll be sent overseas to fight in the war."

I was cold. I was numb. I was dead. I was having a bad dream. It had to be only a bad dream because I could still hear Peter talking.

"The war shouldn't last too long. When I come back, we'll get married and farm both my father's and your Pa's land. We'll have a family and everything will be all perfect."

I didn't care how long or short the war lasted. It was causing us to separate. We, who had just become one. We, who were young and had our whole wonderful lives and plans ahead of us. We, who were living, no matter how meager; we had life and dreams and plans and hopes and love. War was tearing all that away from us.

I started to shiver. I started to cry. I clung to Peter and he to me. For his sake, I wanted to stop the steady flow of tears but I couldn't. Devastation, depression, loneliness were beginning to creep in. I continued to cling to the only person who ever meant anything so dear to me—outside of Ma and Pa, of course.

I clung to him prolonging the inevitable. Finally, with much difficulty, many sobs, and heavy hearts we somehow managed to get back to the road that ended at our lane. By now night had fallen, dark, with only a few stars. Our future was darkened with only a few shiny glimpses of what still may be ahead.

I wanted to walk Peter home even though I knew it probably would be a stupid thing to do. So at the pile of dirt we all used for games and good times, Peter gave me his last long passionate kiss, a gentle caress, and a warm tight embrace. Then he was gone into the night.

I stood still listening to his fading footsteps. I stood long after they had gone from my hearing. My wet face was cold; my whole being was cold. As I came face to face with reality, I discovered a heavy wind had caused clouds to cover the stars. Blowing through my thin blouse it chilled my outer body. Sensibility told me to return to the house. There was no more need to stand out in the cold, windy night. Peter was no longer physically with me, but I knew in spirit he would never leave me.

CHAPTER 19

The wind and clouds brought our first snow of the season, keeping us indoors and busy keeping the fire going. I had no life in me until a beautiful thought came into my mind. Maybe there was life in me. Even now growing from the tiny seed that I hoped, I prayed, that Peter had planted. What if there was a little Peter growing inside of me. Life could be bearable with something that wonderful to look forward to.

I didn't dare hope too much for fear of disappointment, but I did hope, I did pray, and I did dream. They were all dashed to the ground about seventeen days after Peter's departure when I discovered my periods had returned. I grabbed my coat and scarf and ran to the cave. There wasn't too much snow but it was cold and the usual wind was about the country.

Everything was as we left it. That wonderful day came flooding back, filling my mind with pleasant memories. I lay down on the old blanket hoping to get a scent of Peter. The wind that robbed so much from Pa, from Ma, had now robbed that last tiny bit of Peter.

I couldn't hold back any longer; I let the tears flow. All my disappointment and heartache was finally set free from inside. I cried, I sobbed, I took big sighs, and then started all over again until I lay there weak. I began thinking of all the others that were left behind by their 'men'–mothers, (Mrs. DeJong had already lost a son through death. What was she feeling?), wives, daughters, little brothers, sisters, (Olga must be missing him too.)

I stood up, took the blanket, folded it, placed it, and all the other little objects in the cave into the metal box. I placed it in its corner wondering when, if ever, that box would be opened again by one of us.

Ellen's Story

Taking one last look at our 'love nest' I slowly walked home. I had come to terms with myself. I had to accept the fact I had no big Peter or no little Peter to keep me company. But I still had Olga. She was close to Peter and through her and with her we could keep Peter close to us. At least his spirit would always be near.

I also had Ma and Pa. Pa was getting worse though. Ma did everything for him—feed, bathe, and help him to the biffy. His cough was constant, racking his body, at times, with spasms. Sometimes there would be blood in his phlegm.

So that is how we started the winter of '39—down in the mouth but knowing in our hearts we had to carry on. Peter would have wanted us to. All the other sons, husbands, and fathers probably felt the same way.

Christmas approached. I made a chain out of old Christmas wrap and newspaper. I found the old Christmas cards we had received years ago when cards and stamps were affordable and hung them on a string across the top of the living room windows. I splurged and bought some extra sugar to make sugar cookies spreading wild cranberry jelly on top. Mr. DeJong sent us a big roasting chicken, and Ma made mashed potatoes with peas and carrots mashed together. All in all, for us, it was a little more pleasant than in past years except for that empty spot inside me.

The real excitement came on Boxing Day when Olga trudged up the road to show us her shiny, sparkling engagement ring that Tom had given her.

We were all so happy for her. Pa was able to smile a bit and give her his blessing before he had to cough again. Ma and I hugged her and hugged her, all three of us sporting smiles that covered our faces. I'm sure Olga's eyes shone brighter than the stars in the sky. Of course, she talked all the time in her bubbly way that made everyone else feel bubbly too.

Then she became very quiet and came near to me. "Ellen, I've been very selfish, reveling in my own happiness. Please forgive me for I've left your good news till last. We received word from Peter and this small note just for you."

With trembling hands, I took that lifeline and held it close to my heart. Quivering, I thanked her and again hugged her with all the strength I had. "I'll read it later, then tell you what he said," I told her.

"Oh, I don't think there is anything in that note that is meant for our ears. You just cherish it and keep it to yourself," Olga said with eyes that said, "I know you two love each other." I blushed.

After Ma and Pa went to bed, I sat by the fire with the coal oil lamp near on the table and read:

My darling Ellen.

As I write I can vividly see your face framed by your fair hair tied beneath your ears and hanging softly over your breasts. I think of the first time I opened your blouse to cover you with you hair calling you my Lady Godiva. You are still my lady, Lady Ellen.

There is not much to tell yet. In Regina I was sworn in, had my hair cut real short, issued a uniform, top coat (they call it a "great coat"), toiletries, blanket, pay book and a small Bible all in a duffel bag. We traveled by train to Halifax where we boarded a troop ship. There were approximately two hundred ships that set sail in convoy that day—merchants, fuel tankers, battle ships and escorts. The escorts returned to port after reaching international waters.

We landed in Portsmouth, England on the English Channel where we were sent to barracks. Here we will train in the art of killing. It's nicer to call it the "art of self-defense". Old Frank Tonners enlisted. He must be over forty-five years old at least. He was in the first war so he won't see too much of the actual battlefield.

I can't promise when I'll write again. They keep us pretty busy. There is lots to learn. I've met a lot of swell "blokes" as the English call each other.

90

Ellen's Story

A world of hugs and kisses till we meet again.
All my love.
Peter

xoxoxoxoxoxoxoxoxo

Tears misted my eyes, sad but happy tears. He had arrived there safe and would write again. I looked for an address so I could write to him. It wasn't on the note so I assumed it was on the envelope that the DeJongs received. I was sure they would give it to me.

I handled the note for some time thinking his hands also touched this paper. This little piece of paper would keep me going until I received another one. How soon, I wondered, would that be. I looked at the date—it was the end of October. Two months for this note to go from there to here.

With the excitement of Olga and Tom's spring wedding and the promise of more notes from Peter—whenever—our two families survived the winter.

When spring came, Ma and I decided to plant a garden again, especially potatoes. Opening a sealer of vegetables or wild fruit during the winter made us feel like rich folks.

The day we started planting was a warm one with a gentle breeze promising blue skies ahead. Pa wanted to go outside. I packed the rocking chair out to the garden then helped Ma 'walk' Pa to the chair. Easing himself into the chair, he started to cough again. The coughing passed. Pa leaned back in the chair exhausted. With one eye on Pa, we went to work.

Planting seeds takes a fair bit of attention, so much so we almost forgot about Pa until he called out anxiously, "Catherine."

We both looked up just in time to see Pa topple forward onto the grass. I reached Pa first. I rolled him over on his back just as a deathly gurgle sounded in his throat and an unpleasant aroma arose. I knew Pa was no longer of this world.

Because of Ma's heftiness, she was all out of breath by the time she reached our side.

I looked up at her. She saw the tears. "Ellen, he's not...he's not...is he?" she stammered.

A slight positive nod of my head brought her to her knees covering Pa with her huge shaking frame. A true Irish woman, she wailed, she cried, she wept.

Once again the DeJongs rescued us from a dilemma. Tom and Mr. DeJong dug a grave beside the 'holy spot' and built a coffin from some of the stall boards in the barn. Ma was sure Pa would have wanted a priest at his burial but there was no money for that. Tom graciously offered to say a few "Hail Mary's" he had learned somewhere along the way, and Ma accepted his offer.

On a cool spring morn, we laid Pa beside the 'holy spot', the spot that still remained a mystery to me.

I finished planting the garden while Ma moped. She didn't cry anymore, she just mourned. As much as I missed Pa and would continue to miss him, I had Olga's wedding to think about that was coming soon. To be with Peter's family was almost as good as being with Peter.

Besides, Olga had asked me to be her maid of honour.

CHAPTER 20

It was raining when I woke up on the morning of Olga's wedding. Such a disappointment since we had planned everything to be outside. Their house was large and would accommodate the invited guests, but the crepe paper flowers that we so painstakingly made on so many evenings and Sundays would look nicer in their garden rather than in the house.

Plans were for me to come around noon to help put up the decorations and to help with any other little last minute things. It was with great joy that I walked the mile to the DeJongs as the sun had come out not too long before. With the ceremony at 4 pm., the lawn should be dry and the crepe paper roses and streamers would look lovely among the spruce trees that dotted their front lawn.

As most girls who were to be part of the wedding party, I thought, "What will I wear?" With the depression and the 'Dirty Thirties'—as people were beginning to call the 1930's—just barely in the past and a war going on in Europe there wasn't much money anywhere to spend on fancy bridal ware.

'Making do' was one of the many things we learned during hard times. Ma took her prettiest dress of pale blue rayon jersey and made it over into a simple but attractive creation.

"But, Ma," I protested when she first suggested the idea, "that's your only pretty dress."

"Yes, I know, Ellen. But with Pa gone when am I ever going to wear it again? The color suits your fair hair and skin and you'll look lovely. I'll do your hair in braids then make rosettes at your ears. My black sandals should fit you nicely."

I felt like a queen as I walked through the front door of DeJong's house, across their veranda, down the steps, and then on toward the red and white crepe paper arch. Mrs. DeJong had picked a lovely pinkish peony from her garden to pin on my dress as a corsage. Her own carnations were stuck in the lapel holes of Tom and his brother Alvin's suits. Both husky farm men, they looked uncomfortable in their almost too small suits and ties. I'm sure they felt as if they were being strangled.

Reaching the arch, I turned to face the house. Olga dressed in her mother's wedding gown and carrying a small bouquet of roses from her mother's rose bush, traveled the same path on the arm of her proud father. The ceremony began, and as Tom shakily slipped the gold band on Olga's finger I had the fleeting thought: *Would Peter shake like that or would he be his usual calm self?*

I stole a glance at Ma and Mrs. DeJong who were sitting on comfortable chairs on the veranda. Both sets of eyes were misty. I wondered if Ma was thinking of Pa, if Mrs. DeJong was thinking of her two absent sons or were they both thinking of the days they sat together on that same veranda drinking tea or lemonade while Olga and I played with our dolls beneath these very trees. So long ago that was. So much water had gone under the bridge.

A few pictures were taken, and then the feast and revelry began. While the thirty-odd guests were settling the roast beef, turkey etc., Mr. DeJong invited Tom's father to his shop. "I've got a little something I want to show you." And then he winked.

Soon there were other men having a look at this 'little something' and even a lady or two ventured into Mr. DeJong's shop. As the evening wore on, I began to think this 'little something' must be pretty funny because anyone who saw it sure laughed a great deal.

I was sitting with Mrs. DeJong and Ma when Mr. DeJong came up to us laughing and saying to Ma, "No disrespect, Catherine, but I'm sure Kelly would have really enjoyed himself tonight."

Ma weekly smiled and answered, "Yes, I think he would have."

Ellen's Story

Mrs. DeJong bristled and said to her husband, "Horace, I think you and your friends should stay out of the shop. You've had enough."

"Ah, Zelda. Don't take on so. Olga is the only daughter I was able to walk down the aisle and I'm celebrating. The depression robbed me of that privilege for the other two."

"But, Horace," Mrs. DeJong argued, "what will the church people think?"

Mr. DeJong leaned over close to his wife's face and said, "They can kiss my you-know-what."

"Horace!" Mrs. DeJong was aghast.

Mr. DeJong straightened up and walked away laughing.

The little episode struck me as quite funny. I wanted to laugh but didn't dare. Ma would have reprimanded me for being rude. But I had never seen Mr. DeJong so jolly, laughing and having a good time. Nor Mrs. DeJong so serious. I could see both sides. Of course, you have to be sensible and polite when you are in the midst of others, but we also needed to laugh. Not only our two families but also everyone had been robbed of pleasure for so long it was time to get out and celebrate life. A wedding was a good place to do just that.

But why did everything seem to be so funny? Some things that were said made no sense at all. I asked Mrs. DeJong what was making her husband so happy.

"Ellen," she said taking a deep breath, "you have just witnessed a man on his way to becoming very drunk."

"What do you mean?"

"Horace, I mean Mr. DeJong, and his friends have been going into the shop for a nip of moonshine, rot gut, homemade whiskey. Let me tell you, child, like I told my own, never drink a drop of that stuff. It makes you silly in the head, making you do stupid things."

Dianne Osborne

I noticed Ma seemed to be having a difficult time with her emotions. I asked, "Are you okay, Ma?"

"Ah, yes. Yes, I'm okay. I'm just getting a little tired," Ma answered.

"Oh, Catherine," Mrs. DeJong exclaimed apologetically, "I'm so sorry. I haven't been looking after my most special guest. Can I do anything for you?"

"Actually, Zelda. I really would like to go home."

"Well, then. I'll take you home. I've just learned to drive the car. I'm sure I'll do a better job than Horace will at this moment."

I stood up saying, "I'll go with you, Ma."

"No, Ellen, stay and enjoy yourself with the young people. Olga always has enjoyed your company. Somebody can take you home later," Mrs. DeJong encouraged me.

Ma confirmed Mrs. DeJong's suggestion.

I joined the others, drank a glass of fruit juice, nibbled on some goodies, and shared a laugh or two. But the absence of Peter was paramount.

Twilight was falling. Soon guests would leave and Olga and Tom would go off by themselves to revel in each other's company, to start a new life, to become one. Maybe they already had had that pleasure just as Peter and I had. That thought made me want to leave earlier and on my own. To see them leave together would hurt too much.

I said my good-byes, gave my best wishes, declined a ride home, and began the mile long walk.

I could still hear laughter in the distance when I stopped on the side of the road. I removed Ma's high-heeled sandals that were making my feet ache. I removed my one and only pair of silk stockings. The rubber sealer rings that held them up just above my knees were cutting into my leg uncomfortably. I tucked the stockings and rings into Ma's beaded evening purse, slipped my fingers through the slings of the sandals to enjoy a leisurely stroll home under a starry sky.

I found Ma sitting on Pa's couch, something she never had done before. She was sitting there staring out the window.

Cautiously, I sat down beside her. She slipped her arm around my shoulder. I laid my head on her ample bosom and my arm on her ample abdomen.

"Thinking about Pa?" I quietly asked.

She kissed the top of my head then laid her head there and said, "Yes, I'm thinking about Pa. No doubt you are thinking of Peter."

We sat there still and quiet both thinking and both staring through the window into the darkness from the darkness.

Finally, I could hold it in no longer. I had to tell someone. "Ma," I whispered.

"Yes, my girl."

"Peter and I came together just before he left for Europe," I blurted out.

"Yes, Ellen, I know. Pa realized it first and then confided in me saying, "Katie, me love, I'm sure Ellen and Peter know what it's all about. When you stormed out the house a few weeks later, we knew for sure. It was wrong. The wedding night is the time for those things to happen, but we were and I am glad you became a woman. You'll be able to understand life so much better now. Pa had wanted to give you and Peter his blessing as he did Olga and Tom. I guess there are some things that aren't meant to be. Sometimes it is hard to accept what life hands out to you but it is better if we do. Here I am preaching about accepting fate when I'm having a hard time believing Pa is gone."

"That's okay, Ma. I understand. It hasn't been all that long ago Pa left us. You still have me to love you."

"I love you, too, Ellen."

97

Again we sat cuddled together. My mind wandered over the day. It had been fun preparing for it, but also it was lots of work. Mrs. DeJong looked tired.

"Did you notice Mrs. DeJong had quite a nasty cough?" I said breaking the silence.

"Yes, I did and mentioned it to her. She said the doctors don't quite know the cause of it."

We were quiet again falling asleep in each other's arms. Just at that moment that unconsciousness takes over, I felt closer to Ma than I ever had before. The closeness lasted until her death.

CHAPTER 21

Olga and Tom started life together in a tiny little house they
rented in town. Olga continued to work at the store, Tom at
the elevator, and I at Mrs. DeJong. My day at Mrs. Walkers was
changed to Wednesday. Mr. Black gave Olga, now Mrs. Parker, that
particular day off. Since Mrs. DeJong could now drive their car, she
would take me to Mrs. Walker and herself to Olga for a day's visit.
Upon finishing at Mrs. Walker I would walk over to Olga for a short
visit before Mrs. DeJong brought me home.

I missed Olga. I cherished the short visits but longed for one
evening or a Sunday afternoon chat. I wondered if we would ever
share another intimate 'sisterly' experience again. There seemed to be
so many changes occurring.

Ma and I harvested the garden we were planting the day Pa died.
We made pickles and preserves and chutneys and made sure the cold
cellar would be perfect for keeping the potatoes, carrots, and turnips.
We picked berries during the summer and canned them. When there
was a cold nip in the air, we laid in a good supply of coal and wood.
When the snow covered the ground, we were ready for it.

But we didn't account for the time that was all of a sudden on
our hands. Ma did a great deal of moping around during the summer
but still kept herself from complete devastation. The household
chores took only a short time in the morning, leaving the rest of the
day looming far into the distance. On my days at Mrs. DeJong and
Mrs. Walker, her days dragged even more.

Mrs. Walker, that sweet wonderful elderly lady I shall never forget, always asked about Ma. When I told her how Ma was so listless,
she gave me a suggestion, and I readily grabbed at it.

The Red Cross was supplying yarn to knit socks and mitts for
our boys overseas. They needed knitters. One Wednesday afternoon

when Mrs. DeJong brought me home, I was loaded down with two brown paper shopping bags containing yarn, directions, and needles.

Anxiously, I started my first sock that evening. Ma waited until the next day but did very little. She refused to knit on Sunday as that was the Lord's Day, a day of rest. When I came home from DeJongs on Monday, she still had not made too much progress.

As I knitted throughout the winter, I would wonder, "Will these be the socks Peter will be wearing? Will these be the mitts that will keep Peter's hands warm?" It was a great incentive to get as many socks and mitts done as I could.

Although Ma was a quick and a good knitter, I noticed she would only get one sock done to my two. Many times she would sigh and rest her hands and work on her lap to just stare into space.

It was hard for me to know if she was missing Pa so much it was taking her mind off of her work or was she just tired. She seemed to be tired much of the time. Her weight hampered most of her movements. Climbing the stairs to bed at night would find her breathing heavy as she hefted her large body up that last step.

Finally, we decided to bring her bed downstairs to a corner of the living room. It made it crowded, but there was only the two of us, and very few if any visitors came so we managed. I rather liked the idea of sleeping alone upstairs. For once in my life, I had real privacy, real privacy to read Peter's few letters over and over again. Most of them were short, telling of small battles and of the nights out on the town with his newfound buddies and of some of the conditions he had to endure. One letter went like this:

Dearest Ellen,

It's been one hell of a week. Others went through worse hell than I did. Maybe some are there permanently but I hope they are in heaven instead. I heard by the grapevine that we won this last battle but by the amount of mutilated and dead bodies I had to step over and sometimes move I'm not sure if the results were true. But that's not for me to say.

The rain here in Europe is more of a drizzle, sometimes heavier than others but not a strong down pour like we have on the prairies. When it rains it's a soaker. Such was the kind of morning we left to go to the front lines. I climbed into the back of the troop truck, found a corner, settled down with a cigarette—yes, I started smoking. It settles the nerves—then promptly fell asleep. I can't help but think that the catnap saved my life. Others didn't sleep. They chewed their nails or chained smoked showing their nervousness. I'm not sure how many of those lived or died and I could have died as well even with the snooze. It sounds feasible. Maybe it just wasn't my time.

The battle progressed. By the second day we reached the bottom of a hill. Small canons, ammunition and other supplies had to be hauled up manually. With two days of rain soaking the hill, hundreds of feet and metal wheels on the canons it wasn't long before the hill was a mountain of mud and slime especially after a hand grenade exploded in our midst to mix blood and guts and brains with the rain and urine.

I'm sorry if I'm upsetting you and I don't want you to think I'm being a cry-baby. The newspapers don't always tell it how it is. I've been here over a year now. The end is too far in the future to speculate.

Otherwise I'm fine. Tired today but should be able to rest up enough to be of some good at the next battle.

Say "hello" to your Ma. Love you.

Peter

xoxoxoxoxo

CHAPTER 22

His letters had to be short as he was allowed only so much paper per letter. Many times he couldn't tell his exact location. That would have been too dangerous if by some chance his letters fell into enemy hands. Towards the spring of 1941, I received a letter written so small I had to use a magnifying glass to read it. This is what he wrote following his very short greeting:

The night was dark but clear. Many stars, no moon. About seven of us were taking refuge on one side of a freestanding brick wall that had at one time been part of a house. Flares were shot into the sky by the enemy to try to get glimpses of our battalion's position. Immediately following the flares, grenades and small canon fire would explode close to us shaking our "protective" wall. Our lieutenant realized we couldn't stay for fear of the wall collapsing.

"But where would we go?" one private asked.

"Just across the road is a graveyard. In the center is a crypt. If we can reach that and get inside we would be safe. Most crypts go quite a way into the ground."

"It's so black we can't see where we are going," argued another private.

"As soon as a flare goes up and begins to die out we'll make a run for the tombstones to hide behind. Once there we can feel our way to the crypt," the lieutenant assured everyone.

The corporal disagreed. He felt it safer to stay where we were.

Tight-lipped and with authority the lieutenant ordered, "When the next flare goes up we're moving."

It wasn't long before we could obey his order. There was a ditch near the wall that had to be jumped due to water in it followed by a short but steep incline to the top of the road. After crossing the road we found another ditch. This one had brambles in it that hid a three-foot fence we had to hurdle over. Some of us stumbled, some fell but we all made it to the tombstones. Another flare helped us to the crypt.

Ellen's Story

Eager to get inside we hadn't noticed until later that the lock on the black iron gate had been shot open.

Black as Toby's—ahem—our lieuy lit his cigarette lighter. Stealthily we made our way down the circular stairs keeping close to the walls. Names of deceased loved ones flickered on the brass plates of the burial niches.

I was right behind the lieuy when he suddenly stopped about fifteen steps down from the top. I saw it at the same time as he did at which time he immediately extinguished his lighter.

It was a hand, palm down, about four steps from us. Part of a greatcoat sleeve also was visible. It looked as if the person attached to it could be sitting and resting.

Our pistols already in our hands we covered the lieutenant as he slowly felt his way around the curve, the rest of us following at close quarters. Our shots echoed the lieutenants then cautiously we lit our lighters.

There lay five dead German soldiers all sprawled helter-skelter over the steps. However, it wasn't our bullets that had killed them. They had been dead about twelve hours.

At that point the lieutenant ordered someone to stand guard at the gate. Relief would come in an hour's time.

Being away from the latticed door we all could now ignite our lighters. With cocked pistols pointed at the corpses we precariously made our way past the bodies down to the very bottom which was the equivalent to being four stories underground.

Now we could relax somewhat. We lit our small cooking flares, made some tea, smoked a cigarette then drew straws to see who was to relieve the guard.

And then it hit us. The corporal was not with us. "Damn fool of a pig." spouted the lieutenant then added a few more choice words.

There was really nothing we could do about him except hope he was just delayed along the way eventually making it to safety. By morning we came to the awful conclusion he had stayed behind like he had wanted to.

Dianne Osborne

Cautiously making our way back up we found the clouds had rolled in bringing a fine mist. The enemy had moved on. We scampered over to our own trucks that were picking up our guys to take them back to camp. The Red Cross truck was over by a red brick wall that had collapsed during the night. They were digging out a body. We knew that the lieutenant would not have to demote the corporal for disobeying orders.

I'm well. Love you, Peter.

These letters were a mixture of comfort and anguish to me, comfort because I knew he was still alive and relatively well. Anguish because he was in danger so much of the time. One wrong move, one miscalculation in timing, one tiny mistake of any kind could mean the end of my world. And what about the DeJongs with one son already gone and two daughters who rarely came to visit.

I thought of how our world had changed in the last six years. The two families interlocking through exchange of labor, through children attending the same school, through Peter and I dating, through Olga and I depending on Mr. DeJong for transportation to get to our jobs and Olga's marriage to Tom. So many good times dampened by the loss of Andrew, of Pa, and now Peter in danger.

Knitting kept me occupied. Not so much in the summer as there was the garden and other outside things to do. In the evening I would sit on the bench against the south side of the shed taking in the blues and pinks of the prairie sunset while I made a little progress on a sock. Ma very rarely joined me. She preferred to sit indoors by the window. I would wave to her when I noticed her work in her lap. Many times she never saw me; she was off in her own little world.

Another change came one Wednesday in the fall. Mrs. Walker finally had to admit defeat. She could no longer care for herself effectively. She succumbed to her family's wishes, moving into the city where they could look after her.

Ellen's Story

That meant my cash job was no longer available. I had saved some money so I bought our winter's supply of coal. We were thankful for a good garden and the milk and eggs from DeJongs.

Still it was going to be a tight winter.

CHAPTER 23

L ife began to deal me a slump. Hindsight showed me it was coming. The excitement of Olga's wedding, no matter the size of it, blocked my view as did the frequency of Peter's letters and the illusion that the war should soon be over bringing him home again at anytime.

I was not alone in my weariness. The whole world was beginning to feel the effects and stress of a war that seemed to drag on and on. By the time Remembrance Day of 1941 rolled around, it was only old men and young boys who accompanied the ladies to the cenotaph for the 'one minute silence' service. Everyone stood in the chill autumn wind showing long faces, thinking of their loved ones overseas and wondering if their 'care' packages would reach their men by Christmas or if it would even reach them at anytime.

By prearrangement I went in to the service with the DeJongs. Even an invitation to Olga's for dinner after did not entice Ma to come along. After making sure the fires were all right with coal handy, I walked down to DeJongs at 9:30 a.m. in the sunshine but with a biting wind that lasted all day.

Dinner at Olga's was pleasant but definitely not cheerful. The reminders of the First World War veterans not returning home saddened our hearts as well as the hearts of the community. We sat around the table chatting, but our minds were on Peter, each loving him in different ways, each hoping he would return to us for different reasons.

Later on that day; I sat with Ma on Pa's lumpy couch. It was a frequent habit of ours to sit together as dusk settled over the yard and house—the house that had so much hope, plans, and potential. Whatever happened to those plans was lost in the wind and the war as well as other circumstances that as yet were a mystery to me.

Ellen's Story

Many times, we sat quietly not saying a word, each lost in our own thoughts. Ma would read a scripture or two and write in her journal before darkness set in. Her entries were short as there were really not too many events in our lives worth writing about.

Her thoughts no doubt were on Pa. How she survived from day to day knowing she would never see him again was a marvel to me. His memory must have weighed heavily on her mind and body as Peter's memory did on mine. At least I knew and felt that I would see Peter again.

Her body, although still large, was becoming flabby. With great difficulty and much wheezing she crawled from the squeaky bed after a night of tossing and turning and coughing. A spring or two would boing as there was very little padding surrounding them. Rings of the springs showed through the thin sheets.

Ma wore an old pair of shoes run down at the backs. These she used as mule slippers, slipping her feet into them to flip-flop into the kitchen. Her threadbare nightgown bellowed out as she settled into her chair. A cup of tea, an egg, and sometimes a piece of toast was her breakfast.

I would place the dishes in the dishpan and cover them with a tea towel. The habit of conserving water that developed during the drought still remained with me. The day's dishes would be done all together after supper.

Rumbling back to her corner of the living room where her bed was, she would stop by the window. Whether the day was sunny or cloudy she would comment on the weather in the same tone of voice followed by a heavy sigh. I remembered as a child how I wondered if the weather had any effect on her and Pa's moods. Watching this ritual, I came to the conclusion that they had eyes for each other only. I was to find out the real truth later.

As for my thoughts as we sat together, they, naturally, turned to Peter. Always my thoughts were on Peter. Doing household chores, I would make believe I was cleaning Peter's house. On long walks through the hayfield or by the ravine, I was accompanied by Peter's spiritual presence. Nearing our love nest, I would turn away. I could not bring myself to go there. There was too much ache in my heart, too much ache in my loins to be there alone. Once in the house, I would go to my room to fill my aching, empty arms with my pillow.

Mondays at the DeJongs were like heaven. Although we rarely spoke of Peter for fear of emotions getting the best of us, we shared a companionship that was next to kin. I was sure Mr. and Mrs. De-Jong felt that someday I would be kin.

On this Remembrance Day evening, we had a little more to talk about as we listened to the wind in the eaves, the comforting roar of the fire, and the soothing singing of the kettle on the stove.

"Olga was telling me that she noticed a few of the younger women were missing from the towns folk crowd. Rumour had it that they too had joined the armed forces."

Ma, who felt women should stay at home, was shocked, exclaiming, "Whatever for?"

"I've noticed in the papers that women are needed in offices to do the accounts, statistics, and many more things that need to be typed out and sent to various places. That's one job they do. I've seen pictures of nice looking ladies in their trim uniforms. It kind of appeals to me."

"Ellen, really. Well, I never."

"Don't worry, Ma. I'm not healthy enough to join up. But if I could join I'd have to be a cook's helper or janitor or something like that because I don't have enough education. I don't think I'd care to work in the factories making ammunition."

"I guess you wouldn't." Ma was scandalized that women would do such things and have to wear pants as well.

"But, Ma, you shouldn't get all worked up about it. If this war is to be over, we all have to pitch in to make life easier for the fellas fighting–like we do knitting socks. Many women have gone overseas as nurses and medical aides. Without their help, links in the system would be missing. I don't know a whole lot about women in the forces, just what I read in the week-old newspaper Mr. DeJong brings. I guess it's like team work, Ma."

"I guess you're right," Ma resignedly said. "There's been so many things happen since we came to Canada. So many changes..." She sighed, as her mind seemed to wander a little.

In a moment, her mood changed. She asked, "How are the De-Jongs? How are Olga and Tom getting on?"

"Well, Ma, in general the DeJongs are fine. Tom seemed to be proud of his little corner of the world. Olga cooked a lovely roast beef dinner. Mr. DeJong definitely agreed the beef was good because after all it came from his farm. We all had a little chuckle over his boasting. The chuckling brought on a coughing fit from Mrs. De-Jong. Ma, I'm really worried about her. She coughs like Pa did. I sure hope the doctors can help. Maybe then we'll know why Pa coughed so much."

"I'm sorry to hear that, Ellen. And, yes, I guess it would be nice to know why Pa coughed so much. But then again, what good would it do? It won't bring him back again." She stared into the black windowpane.

CHAPTER 24

By the end of November, the days were getting noticeably shorter. As I walked to DeJongs that Monday morning a couple of weeks after Remembrance Day, dawn was just beginning as the hands of the clock climbed towards the eighth hour of the morning. There still wasn't much snow for that time of the year but enough to make walking a little difficult as I made my own tracks down the road.

Turning into DeJong's driveway I noticed car wheel tracks coming out of their lane and turning towards town. Strange that Mr. DeJong had to go to town so early, I mused.

Following the car track, I began to feel uneasy. The dense grove of shelterbelt poplar tress protected the yard from the gentle breeze that was moving the grey clouds around. This left a heavy stillness in the air. The crunch of my boots on the snow and the impatient lowing of the cattle in the barn were the only sounds. Any minute, I expected Mr. DeJong to burst forth from the porch door with a hearty "Good morning, Ellen" as he made his way to the barn to feed his animals.

Approaching the house, a closed door greeted me with a white paper that had some writing on it. Soon I realized it was addressed to me. It said:

"Ellen, I'm sorry to have caused you to walk all the way for nothing but Mrs. DeJong took terribly ill today so I drove her into the doctor again. We won't be needing you on Monday. We'll let you know when you can come again. Once again, I'm sorry for your walk for nothing.

It was signed "Mr. DeJong" and dated the day before which was Sunday.

Ellen's Story

I didn't feel that my walk was for nothing. At least I knew Mrs. DeJong had seen a doctor and that she needed to see him again. I was distressed at the news that she was poorly but glad she was in the doctor's hands.

But where was she? There was no hospital in town, and they had left yesterday.

Standing there with a hundred questions going through my mind, the rattle of Tom's ten year-old truck came to my ears. I left the step moving towards him as he came into the yard. He stopped a few yards from the house.

The look of sadness on his face as he stepped out onto the ground stopped me in my tracks. I was almost afraid to say anything, but I needed to know.

Without a greeting of any kind, I asked, "How's Mrs. DeJong?"

He put his hands in his jacket pockets hunching his shoulders and sighing deeply. With his head bowed and eyes on the toes of his boots, I could hardly decipher his words of, "Not very good."

Becoming mobile, I stepped forward putting my hand on his arm. "Oh, Tom, I'm so sorry to hear that. Is she with Olga?"

Tom sighed again as he walked over to the front fender of his truck. Leaning on it, he said with eyes still downcast, "Let's put it this way. Olga is with her."

Finally looking at me, he continued. "The doctor felt he could not do anything more for her so he had Mr. DeJong take her to the city to the hospital. Before they left, they came to the house to see if I could do the chores here at the farm. Olga wanted to go with them so we all agreed it would be a good idea."

We both stood silently looking at the ground, at the sky, just anywhere. I broke the silence saying, "Well, I'm glad Olga is with her. I'm glad she is getting extra care. I just hope she will be better soon.

111

"Yeah, we all hope so too."

Another small silence before I said, "I guess there's nothing left for me to do here so I'll go home. Ma won't be happy to hear the news. She'll probably read a few extra scriptures tonight. That's what she usually does when she's upset."

"I guess that's good," Tom said. "Well, I better feed the cows and horses. I imagine they are hungry."

Turning to leave, I stopped again to ask, "Could you let us know how things are when you find out?"

"Oh, sure," Tom said from in front of his truck. "Thanks for coming."

And so we parted.

No word came for quite a few days. Ma and I were hanging onto the old saying "No news is good news". It wasn't the case this time.

CHAPTER 25

It was quite a few days later, maybe twelve to fifteen days later, when Mr. DeJong and Tom came driving up our lane. I grabbed my shawl from the peg in the porch and ran out to greet them. Their faces told me they were not bringing good news.

Oblivious of the ever-present wind–this one being a cold one as it passed over the snow infested land–I stood huddled waiting for Mr. DeJong to get out of the car

Slowly he came towards me. Knowing he didn't have to wait for me to ask the question, he came straight to the point. "Mrs. De-Jong has passed away."

The wind had nothing to do with the coldness that spread through my body. "I...I...I didn't think...didn't think she was that sick," I stammered.

"It was tuberculosis. It developed and traveled fast. It does that in some people, especially if not looked after in the beginning."

"How...how is...Olga taking this?" I managed to get out between chattering teeth.

Mr. DeJong looked at the snow. "Of course she is devastated as we all are. The worst for her is that she won't be able to come to her Mother's funeral."

Surprised, I asked, "Why not?"

"Well," Mr. DeJong spoke slowly deciding what he had to tell me, "the doctors examined Olga and me after diagnosing my wife. I'm clear, but Olga has tuberculosis too."

"No! No, Mr. DeJong, that can't be." He seemed to be able to hear my mind saying, "No, she can't die too." for he said, "Olga's disease is just at the beginning stage. She has a small spot on her lung. With medication and complete rest she will get better. She will have to spend two years in a sanitarium with no visitors for the first

113

while. She was admitted soon after we discovered the illness which was not long after we went to the city."

Speechless, I took a look at Tom who hadn't got out of the car. He didn't look around, just straight ahead, afraid that movement might bring on more tears, tears that were not to be shed in public.

"Oh, Oh," was all I could say. My tone was flat like my feelings at the moment. I started to shiver as the wind brought back reality. Mr. DeJong noticed it.

"You had better get back into the house before you catch your death of cold."

My manners also came back, and I extended my hand in sympathy. He took it in both of his hands saying, "The funeral is on Thursday from the church in town."

Thanking him, I replied, "As much as I would like to be there I don't think I can make it."

We both knew that he would have to be my transportation. There was relief in his face and voice as he said, "I understand."

They left, and I slowly returned to the house.

As darkness fell, we lit the lamp. Even the gentleness of twilight would have been heavy on our spirits. Then again Ma needed the light to read her scriptures, tonight the number being many.

The hulk of Ma's body as I sat close to her comforted me in a way that no words could. Our companionship was such that we found consolation in just sitting, our arms and thighs touching. Even Pa's shabby and tattered old couch did not give us any discomfort as it brought his spirit closer to us.

Ma read her scriptures to herself, breaking in periodically whispering little prayers. Physically, we were close, but we each were in our own little worlds, my thoughts being as numerous as her scriptures.

Ellen's Story

After they left, I assumed Tom had helped Mr. DeJong with the chores and then possibly had a light supper with him. Eating probably didn't really appeal to either one of them; they did it out of necessity. After those things were done, Tom would have gone home to spend a lonely evening alone, one of many yet to come.

My mind conjured up the vision of Tom's rigid face as he sat in Mr. DeJong's car. I pictured him sitting at his kitchen table, maybe tapping is fingers absentmindedly on the luncheon cloth that Olga had spread to help make the kitchen more cheerful. Maybe he just sat still, envisioning Olga setting the table for two while the kettle merrily whistled on the cooking range. Maybe he had no thoughts at all.

I thought of Tom crawling into a cold empty bed. Pillows don't do much for empty arms. I could attest to that. I envied Tom the one consolation he had–in two years time he would have the love of his life home again to fill his life with happiness and his arms with love. I knew in my heart Peter would be mine when he came back. The agony for me was when would he return? Or worse yet–something I refused to think about–will he ever come back?

I sympathized with Tom for we were almost in the same situation.

I reprimanded myself then for being so selfish as Mr. DeJong's sorrowful face came into my mind's view. Tonight he will also crawl into a cold empty bed. As with Ma, he will do that for the rest of his life. No more will he able to hold her, no more to hear her gentle laugh or an infrequent scolding. I smiled in spite of myself as I remembered the moonshine episode at Olga's wedding. Nor more will he be able to… well, there will be so many 'no mores'.

Mr. DeJong will be busy for the next few days. No doubt his older daughters will be home to give him a hand with funeral preparations. I really did want to go to the funeral, but I would need Mr.

115

DeJong to take me. He will have enough to do without being concerned about me. There was Ma to think about too. The weather might be nasty; to leave her on her own with the fires would be dangerous and, of course, I wouldn't know how long I would be.

Then there was the letter that Mr. DeJong will have to write to Peter. How will Peter be able to handle the shock of this terrible news? He deals with death almost every day, but this is different. He left behind a healthy mother. Now of a sudden, she is no longer of this world. Hopefully, his corporal or lieutenant or whomever is in charge will give him a leave of absence so he can get used to the idea; so he can grieve, so he can get his wits about him again. How I longed to hold him, to comfort him, to help in his grieving.

I let my mind wander over the years that we knew the De-Jongs–the good times, the sad times, the help they had extended us as newcomers, the kindnesses, the thoughtfulness, the understanding of our situation, and the supplying of a job for me even though I'm sure Mrs. DeJong could have done without me. Well now, there is another 'no more'. This time it is for me–no more job.

Mr. DeJong will definitely not need me now that it will be only him there. Besides, it would not look good for a young girl to be housekeeping by herself for a widower. To find a housekeeping job elsewhere was out of the question due to the transportation problem. I would never ask Mr. DeJong to take me into town for that reason. For a matter of fact, "I may as well start right now getting used to the idea of going to town on foot." I occupied my mind on how I would manage that situation.

Ma's coughing broke into my thoughts. Was Mrs. DeJong's cough like Ma's? I tried to think back, to compare, but no one person's cough is the same as another's even if they both have a cold or whatever. The thought did come to me that maybe Ma has the same thing Mrs. DeJong had. But how could I get Ma to a doctor? How would I be able to pay him? What little money I saved from my summer jobs will only last the winter. What would happen in the spring, I didn't know. As pressing as it was, I had to leave that thought alone for tonight. Too much had happened in the last two to three weeks.

The next day, as Ma paused at the window to comment on the day, she called to me instead, "Ellen, there is smoke coming from the DeJong's trees."

I hurried to her side to see what made her so anxious. As I watched the smoke rise, I tried to picture in my mind its exact location. Then I remembered. "I don't think we have too much to worry about. Andrew's grave is in that area. Mr. DeJong and Tom are burning wood and coal to thaw the ground so they and, I hope, some other neighbours can dig Mrs. DeJong's grave."

"Of course. Why didn't I think of that?" She continued on her way to her bed to dress herself.

"Ummm…. Maybe I could go to the graveside service. No, I better not. I'll just be in the way," were my thoughts as I returned to my interrupted job.

On Thursday, we watched out our window for life stirring at the DeJongs. Around noon, we saw the hearse turn into their lane, disappearing behind the row of trees that bordered the lane.

As I watched, a few more cars turned in; I couldn't help realizing how different life is going to be. Except for Peter's return and our inevitable marriage (I was so sure of it) association with the DeJongs was going to be sporadic. It will be two years before I would be able to see Olga, to give her a hug, to hear her lively chatter. It would be very inappropriate for me to visit Tom or Mr. DeJong. It would be absolutely frowned on by the citizens of the town. Staying away from them as much as possible would save embarrassment for all concerned. My only contact with that family will be with Peter through our exchange of letters.

117

Dianne Osborne

Rereading his letters helped my day-to-day spirits. How I longed for a new letter. Maybe there was one at the post office even now.

"Well, feet," I said to myself, "as soon as I can see a nice day, we will have to make that trip to town for the mail and a few small groceries that I can carry."

Ellen's Story

CHAPTER 26

It was just a few days before Christmas Day when the sun came out bright and warm. It was one of those days you just couldn't stay inside.

At this time of the year on the prairies the days were very short, the sun not showing his face till almost 9 a.m. and retiring only eight hours later.

The coldest part of any day is at dawn. It takes an hour or so before one can get a good idea of how high the thermometer is going to rise. This meant that it was mid-morning before I made the decision to take that five-mile trek into town.

I told Ma, "I've put wood and coal close to the stove so you will be able to keep the fire going. It will be noon by the time I reach town where I'll do my shopping as quickly as I can. If all goes well, I should be back before sunset at 4:30."

"That's a long day without food, Ellen," Ma said.

"I'll make a cheese sandwich, wrap it in a piece of wax paper saved from the dry cereal box, and put it in my pocket. I'll be thirsty by the time I get home but if you keep the kettle hot it won't be long before a pot of tea can be made. I've taught you in the last six weeks or so how to look after the stove knowing someday I would have to make this trip. Just remember what I showed you, and we'll both be able to sit down to a nice hot drink when I get back."

"How will you carry the groceries?" Ma wanted to know.

"I'll ask the store clerk for a brown paper shopping bag with the cord handle. It is easier carrying a bag from the hands rather than in my arms which I would have to do with the ordinary brown paper bag."

As Ma watched me make my sandwich and pile on layers of clothing–another pair of cotton stockings over the ones I already had

119

on, a cardigan sweater over my wool dress, my long coat, knitted hat, scarf, mittens, and overshoes—she commented, "You are going to be quite stiff and sore tomorrow after your ten-mile walk."

"I know, Ma. My daily walks to DeJong's driveway and back again, sometimes doing it twice and my wanderings along the ravine will make this walk somewhat easier."

"You're so frail, Ellen. What if you slip and fall? You may not be able to get up again. You'll be too tired. What if you break an arm or leg?"

"Ma," I scolded, "stop fretting. I've looked at these aspects many times while we are having our evenings together. There is no other way. We can't depend on the DeJongs anymore; there is only one left and he has enough troubles of his own. I have to do what I have to do."

I gave her a quick hug and kiss as I hurried out the door. I was getting too warm to stay inside with all those extra clothes on. Before I shut the door, I called back, "Read your Bible, Ma, and everything will be alright."

Pa always called walking using "shank's pony'. So I set my 'shank's pony' at a steady pace, not hurrying, not sauntering. As I passed DeJong's driveway, a feeling of sadness swept over me. At this time of the morning, Mr. DeJong would be just finishing his chores and returning to the house. I pictured him taking off his big woolen mittens, his wool peaked cap that had turndown earflaps for colder days and his heavy black woolen coat with a large collar. A scarf around his neck with ends tucked into a pair of braces that held up a pair of heavy woolen trousers he wore over twill pants would stay on, as did the trousers, if he was going to go outside again. Always he took off his rubber overshoes revealing felt and leather lace up boots. The clothing would be hung in the porch but the overshoes were brought to the stove to dry on old newspapers. Coming to the kitchen table, tea and goodies would be waiting for him.

Today and many more days to come, the clothes would be removed as before, but the added job of perking up the fire, putting the kettle on to boil, making the tea, and setting the table would be up to him. He would then sit down all alone to tea and maybe some goodies if he received some from good neighbours or had the ambition to try to make some himself. Maybe it would be a piece of bread or simply some crackers and cheese.

Once I had gone past the yard, my spirits began to lift. It was a beautiful day. As fond as I was of the DeJongs, there was nothing more I could do for them except give them my moral support. It was up to Mr. DeJong himself to make the best of his own situation as I was trying to do in my own life. If I and Ma were to eat, it was up to me to get to town in whatever way I could even if it meant walking.

As I said before, life was going to be different, and today is the first day of my new life, a new adventure.

The warmth of the day and the exertion of my movements caused me to take my mittens off, which I placed in my pockets. Loosening my scarf and unbuttoning the top button of my coat gave me a nice wisp of cooling air. I trudged on, taking note of the fields to my left and right of white desert. Far in the distance 'oases' could be seen—shelterbelts of poplar and spruce trees enclosing family homes of people and livestock. Also in the distance straight ahead of me, the town grew slowly larger. A strange excitement grew in me. I couldn't remember ever coming to town before on my own. Always Pa had gone, sometimes in the summer taking Ma and me. Then it was the DeJongs that brought me in. Today I was on my own.

A little less than a mile from town I took out my sandwich eating it and savouring every bite. Never did a cheese sandwich taste so

121

good. Was it my exercise? Was it the warm yet crisp air? I don't know. It just tasted good.

I folded the wax paper and returned it to my pocket as I entered the town. The road I was traveling on became Main Street. But what a beautiful main street.

Four blocks into the town, the main avenue crossed Main Street. In that intersection there stood a huge spruce tree, really bushy with a tinge of blue, just like out of a storybook. On the top, a shiny star caught the sun's rays reflecting its own rays. Hundreds of candy canes, stockings, wreaths, circles and squares, more stars, gingerbread men, etc. made of wood and painted bright red and green and yellow hung from the many branches. Somewhere in what Pa called this 'land of plenty', the town—even in the hard times we were having—had found yards and yards of silver tinsel. This circled the tree from top to bottom where my eyes caught the sight of a man clad in red and white. Santa Claus was ringing his bells, laughing and handing out brown paper bags to dozens of excited children.

I slowly came closer and watched for a while. Children left while others came, all of them wanting to tell Santa their wishes. All of them shouted "Thank you" and "Merry Christmas" as they joined their parents.

For a moment, there were no children gathered around him. I was about to leave when he beckoned to me.

"Good afternoon, Miss Woods. Nice to see you. Come closer so I don't have to shout."

Shyly, I came forward. "Good afternoon, Santa."

He saw that I was at a loss for words so he took the lead in conversation, and soon I was able to answer sensibly and cheerfully. I was even able to laugh. What a wonderful feeling!

Finally, I had to break the spell. More children were coming; they needed his attention.

Ellen's Story

As I was leaving, he stopped me, handed me two brown bags that he took from one of the many cardboard boxes, and said, "One for you and one for your Ma."

I exclaimed, "I can't accept these. We're not children."

He answered with a twinkle in his eye "You're all children in my sight."

Taking it in that view, I couldn't refuse the bags. With a lump in my throat, I whispered, "Thank you and Merry Christmas from Ma and me."

A fatherly pat on the back sent me on my way with a glad heart.

Clutching my precious brown bags, I was unwilling to let go of this magical moment. I took my time as I headed for the grocery store. On the way, I passed various types of stores each having large windows to display their wares. A variety shop showed glass and ceramic ornaments as well as gaily painted thin china cups and saucers reminding me of the gay lunches I shared with Mrs. Walker. Mannequins in silky, black and sequined dresses posed in clothing store windows. Hardware stores displayed tools for the serious or handyman carpenter. Faux pearls and rhinestone jewelry blinked and shone out of black satin boxes in a barred window display of a jewelry store. The pharmacy held everyone's interest–especially children–as animated elves worked at making toys while an electric train rattled merrily on its track letting out a periodic whistle.

Everywhere there was laughter and gaiety and good spirits; everyone wishing each other "Merry Christmas"and "Happy Holidays." Even I was greeted with heartfelt warmth and well wishes. It became easier for me to return the salutations if I happened to meet a few people I did know in the town. Even those I was not acquainted with said "hello" or at least smiled.

In my wanderings, I came across a second hand shop. A great variety of items adorned its window: toys and tools, china ornaments

123

and dishes, pictureless frames, mirrors and even a few Christmas ornaments and tarnished tinsel. This was a store that my pocket book could handle, but there was nothing that I needed. There were things it would be nice to have but were not necessary.

I started to move on when my eye caught a sparkle. There, in a corner almost lost in all the paraphernalia displayed, was a small box. Nestled in the discolored white satin was a brooch of artificial green and white gems. Was it the magic in the air working on my mind or was it really winking and blinking at me, begging me to take it home to Ma. It would be perfect to fasten her old beige shawl that was constantly slipping from her shoulders.

I hesitated. I was in town to buy groceries not baubles.

"But Ma needs some magic too," I argued with myself. The bauble won the argument. Well, at least until I could find out the cost of it.

A middle-aged lady greeted me pleasantly when I entered. After hearing my request, she exclaimed, "Oh, yes. That is a pretty piece of jewelry, isn't it? A lady brought that in along with some other pieces. Would you like to have a look at those too?"

"No, Madam," I said as kindly as I could. "I'm only interested in the green brooch."

"Well, then, I have to tell you I have a price of 10¢ allotted for that. How does that sound?"

It sounded a bit pricey for a second hand brooch. My mind worked fast–from groceries to Ma's happiness.

"I'll…I guess I'll take it," I said shifting my brown bags so I could get to my change purse in my coat pocket.

"Shall I wrap it for you?" said the lady.

"No. Thank you, anyway. I'll just put it in my pocket."

The transaction being done, I started to leave when I noticed a sled by the door. It looked so much like the one Peter received that

Christmas so long ago when we tried to make ice on the pile of snow covered dirt at the end of our lane. But then all sleds looked so similar.

It felt a little chillier when I stepped out on to the street again. I looked at the clock in the town hall tower.

"It's past three o'clock. I still have groceries to buy and an hour and a half walk home. It will be getting dark by that time, and Ma will be getting worried."

I hurried to the grocery store where Olga used to work and where I would wait for Mr. DeJong to come pick us up. Mr. Black was glad to see me; I was glad he remembered me.

Once my purchases were made–including two mandarin oranges–I looked at the quantity with awe. How am I going to carry it all home? Some of the items were bigger and heavier than I expected.

Mr. Black asked, "Is Mr. DeJong going to pick you up?"

I said, "No. I walked in and have to walk back."

"Oh, dear. Oh, dear. We do have a problem here."

Reality was pushing away the magic of the day. But all was not lost yet. Noisy laughter outside the store attracted my attention. Through the glass door I saw boys heading home pulling their sleds. Their snow-covered clothing and rosy red cheeks told me they had had a great afternoon of sledding just as Olga, Peter, Andrew and I had had that winter day.

Immediately, I remembered the sled in the second hand store.

"Could I leave my things here for a few minutes? I'll be right back."

Before Mr. Black could answer, I was gone hurrying across the street, all the while hoping the sled was still there and hoping it wouldn't cost too much. I didn't have much money left.

"Oh, you're back," the nice lady exclaimed.

125

"Yes, and I want to know how much that sled is by the door."

"Oh, let me see now. It's been here for quite some time. It's been well used as you can see by the bent runners. I'd have to have $1.50 for it."

I dumped my change onto her counter to count it. There was only $1.47. My disappointment must have shown for she said, "Well, now. There's not much paint left on it neither so I guess I could bring down the price a little. Could you give me $1.40 for it?"

"Oh, yes, Ma'am." I quickly put the two pennies and the nickel back in my change purse that went back into my pocket. I ran for the door grabbing the sled on the way. I wasn't going to wait for her to change her mind.

But alas. Once outside, I discovered the sled didn't have a rope to pull it with.

"Never mind. I'll push it if I have to."

Mr. Black was watching for my return. "Well, now, young lady. That was a smart idea."

"Yes, sort of. But it has no rope."

"Just a minute," he said holding up his hand. Disappearing into the back, he returned with a small piece of frayed braided twine.

"This won't last long but long enough to get you home."

Together, we attached the braided twine and tied down my parcels with regular twine. I thanked Mr. Black profusely, wishing him all the best for this joyous season. "And please, pass those greeting on to your family," I added as I left his premises.

"Bless you, Child," I heard him call.

I crossed the street and headed once more for the second hand store. The bell on the door announced my entrance for the third time. The gentle lady was surprised to see me again.

"Oh, hello, again. What can I help you with this time?"

Ellen's Story

"I left in such a hurry I forgot to say thank you for the sled. I appreciate what you did. The sled is certainly going to be a great convenience."

"I'm glad I could help," she said with a warm smile.

I hesitated momentarily, not knowing what else to say so I wished her seasons greetings. She hugged me while she tenderly voiced her well wishes for me.

I trudged up the street that would lead to home while pulling my treasures. My glad heart, lifted spirits, and my renewal of my faith in my fellow man lightened the load. My only worry was that Ma would be worried.

As I approached a side street, I heard voices singing. Despite the lateness of the hour, the music drew me till I came to a church. There on the steps, men and women bundled in mufflers and mittens were singing carols. The church door was open to allow the organ music to be heard by the singers.

Beside the steps on what was the flowerbed in summer was a bed of straw with painted cardboard figures of Mary, Joseph, and the Christ child. It was all so awesome.

I stayed until they finished "Peace on Earth, Goodwill to Men." "Silent Night," sent me peacefully on my way.

The runners of the sled on the packed snow gave out a steady hum, background music for the crunch, crunch of my feet and the beat of my happy heart. My breath emanated from my mouth in steady bursts of tiny flimsy clouds. I could feel my nose and cheeks getting red from the clear, crisp air.

The road between DeJongs and home held only a single footpath made by me on my daily walks. The sled runners were a little wider than the path making my journey a little more difficult. Fatigue that was setting in didn't help matters neither. A light in the distance was the thing that kept me going. I knew Ma had put the lamp in the window just as we had done that other January day when Pa went for coal and supplies with the horses.

About halfway on my narrow path, I suddenly heard an animal's howl. I stopped to see if DeJong's dog was following me. Nothing was behind me. Then I heard it again followed by a couple of yaps.

This was definitely not the sound of a family dog. Besides, the DeJongs and we lived on the west side of the road whereas this sound was coming from the east somewhere further down the ravine.

The sound was eerie in the still moonlight night. It gave me a chill, dulling my senses. Pa's words of wisdom came creeping into my brain: "Don't run. Just walk a little faster. Try not to show fear as an animal can smell it."

Taking a deep breath, I gave the sled a tug to continue home, keeping in mind that as long as I can still hear the coyotes in the distance they are not close to me. All the same, by the time I reached the porch, I was so out of breath from hurrying and worrying, I literally fell onto the kitchen floor.

Ma, having seen me pass by the window where she had been watching 'for hours', according to her, reached the kitchen at the some time.

"Ellen! Ellen," Ma exclaimed.

My breath came too hard for me to answer so I just lay there relishing in the knowledge I was safe at home.

Not understanding, Ma again exclaimed, "Ellen, dear, are you alright?"

This time I managed, "Yes, I'm alright."

"You don't sound alright," Ma complained as she dropped into a kitchen chair.

"Just let me rest a minute," I urged.

"Oh, dear. Oh, dear," Ma lamented. "I knew you shouldn't have gone. It was just too much for you. Oh, why did I let you go?"

I let her rant and rave for a minute longer. Slowly and wearily, I sat up and firmly said, "Ma, Please. You would do better if you made me a cup of tea while I bring in the groceries."

"Oh, Ellen. I'm so sorry. Of course. Of course. I'll do that right away. How thoughtless of me."

She hurried as fast as her huge body allowed her, all the while continuing to be in a state of confusion. Should she be sad I was so tired and worn out or should she be glad I arrived safe back home?

Ma had a big pot of welcome tea made by the time I untied my parcels from the sled to bring them into the porch. I brought the sled in, leaning it against the wall for the time being. I would find a storage place for it later. Rather than hanging my coat up, I laid it over the parcels so the oranges and other freezables would not freeze but stay cool. Tomorrow, I would relive for Ma my excursions of my day, but I would keep secret the brown paper bags from Santa to surprise her on Christmas Day, which was two days hence.

I hungrily drank most of the pot of tea as well as devouring a large baked potato Ma had thoughtfully put in the oven. Ma could think when on her own, but when upsetting events took place or when there was someone else to do the thinking, Ma's brain just didn't function right.

The comforts of home, sweet home—the warmth of the fire, a full tummy, and a loved one for companionship—took control. Before long I was dropping off to sleep sitting at the table. Even though it was early evening, I stoked the fire in the stove, gave Ma her goodnight hug and kiss, and crawled up the stairs and into my bed, snuggling under my well worn blankets and quilts. Peaceful sleep came quickly.

CHAPTER 27

A rattling noise below me penetrated into my brain. As the fog cleared, the reason for the noise became clear—someone was shaking the grates in the stove to let the ashes fall to the ash pan below. I pictured Pa's lean frame bent over the stove placing bits of paper and kindling over the dying embers. Soon he'll have a roaring fire. Then I'll go down.

Poking my nose subconsciously out from under the patchwork, I was surprised to feel warmth. In confusion, I slowly opened my eyes. The sun flooding my room through the south window told me it was almost midmorning. Why was Pa up so late? Ma's voice calling up the stairs, "Ellen, can you get this stove going for me?" also called me back to the present.

Soon the fire was going. We pulled our chairs close to the stove, and, as we had our coffee and toast, I told Ma all about my wonderful day.

I concluded my tale of joy by telling Ma I'd like to do some decorating. "Maybe I'll put a few twigs in a can of coal for a tree. We've got some yarn we can wrap around it for tinsel. There's still some wrapping paper we can cut stars and circles to hang on the branches. We can have some fun doing it, too. Okay?"

Ma seemed to have lost interest halfway through my plans even though I was getting excited again. She enjoyed my story but when it came to doing something—well, that was something different.

When she didn't say anything, I sighed, got up, and went out to the porch to start putting my purchases away.

I reached for my coat and then screamed.

"Ellen, whatever is the matter?" Ma called from the other room.

Ellen's Story

"Ma," I exclaimed, "how in the world did that chicken get there?" For that is what it was that had startled me, a dead featherless, headless chicken hanging from its feet.

"Oh, Ellen, I'm sorry. I forgot to tell you. Mr. DeJong brought that yesterday. He said he had killed and plucked it just before Tom came to say that Mr. DeJong was invited to Tom's parents on Christmas Day. Rather than let it go to waste, he thought we could use it for our Christmas dinner."

"Well," I said calming down. "That was very nice of him. I'm glad he has somewhere to go for Christmas. I'll leave the chicken there till tomorrow morning. I'll stuff it then and put it in the oven. We'll have our meal around four o'clock. Is that okay with you, Ma?"

"Yes, that is okay. Speaking of stuffing, you'll have to clean it first."

"I know, Ma. Rinse it in cold water a couple of times."

"That too, Ellen. But you'll have to remove the innards first."

"What, Ma? You know I've never fully cleaned a chicken before."

"Yes, I know. Neither have I. Pa always did it or else we've always received cleaned chickens from the DeJongs after Pa died and when he was so sick."

All the magic and excitement of Christmas was gone. My stomach churned. All was quiet, which was really nothing unusual, but it seemed to deepen as I stood wishing Pa were here. But Pa wasn't here, and Ma definitely wasn't going to do the job. With a sigh of resignation, I began to prepare for the gruesome job.

Newspapers were spread on the kitchen table, pans of cold water stood ready, knives were sharpened, and the chicken taken from the hook in the porch and placed on the newspapers. First thing to go was the feet. A slit in the rear end revealed slimy purplish blue entrails.

131

Now what? Searching for help through the memories of when Pa did it, I heard him say, "Nothin' to it, Sprig. Just reach your hand in along the breastbone to the neck. Then, using it as a scoop, pull everything all out in one sweep."

I didn't get everything all out at once but most of it. I didn't search for the heart or liver, everything went on to the newspaper. The job had to be done as quickly as possible before I had another mess to clean up.

After a couple of washes in the cold water, I put it in the roaster that I put in the porch to keep cool until the next day.

The mass was wrapped in the newspaper and then into a brown paper bag. Slipping my overshoes and coat on, I took it out behind the barn where I threw everything as far as I could. Being wet, the paper ripped when it landed on the hard wind-blown snow bank. Guts and feet flew every which way.

"Merry Christmas, birds," I said sarcastically out loud and hurried back to the house.

Once all was cleaned up, I decided it really wasn't as bad as I thought it would be, but I didn't eat supper that night.

Later on that evening, when I was making a pot of tea for our bedtime snack, my stomach began to growl. Remembering the oranges and how Pa had surprised us with some, I took them to Ma and said, "I have a surprise for you, Ma. I found an extra nickel on the ground so I bought us a mandarin orange each."

Ma slowly lifted her eyes from her usual evening reading and writing and gave me a horrified look. "Ellen!" she almost screamed.

Stunned at this reception, I hurriedly explained, "Oh, Ma, I didn't find a nickel. If I did I'd try to find its owner. I only meant that I had an extra 5¢ in my pocket so I thought the oranges would be a nice treat for us on this Christmas Eve."

"You're sure you're telling the truth?"

Ellen's Story

"Of course, Ma. Have I ever lied to you before?"

"Well, no. Not that I can recall. I'm sorry I got excited. It's just that...well, someday you'll understand." She reached for the proffered orange.

We ate in silence. We went to bed in silence. I came to the conclusion there was a great deal that I didn't understand including the reason why I couldn't hang on to yesterday's magic no matter how hard I tried.

But I was not to be deterred. Towards morning, I crept downstairs stepping over the third step from the top because it creaked so bad. Knowing the house as I did, in the darkness, I was able to quietly open the drawer of the buffet to retrieve one of Ma's fancy luncheon cloths. This I put on the kitchen table placing the two brown paper bags from Santa and Ma's brooch now wrapped in formerly used tissue paper in the center.

Imagine my surprise when I later returned to the kitchen to fix the fire as well as to prepare breakfast, to find a bulky brown paper parcel added to the collection having my name on it.

When Ma came to the kitchen, we hugged each other exclaiming simultaneously, "Merry Christmas."

We opened our gifts to each other. Ma was more than pleased with the brooch. Pinning her shawl together with it, she declared she would wear it forever.

The wool of the hand knit mitts in my parcel I recognized as an old burgundy colored cardigan sweater Ma wore years ago when she was slimmer. I envisioned her climbing laboriously up the stairs to her former room, bringing it down, ripping it apart and then re-knitting it into mittens for me. All this had to be done when I was out on my walks. It proved my point that Ma could knit fast when necessary.

"You must have had one eye on the knitting and one eye on the window watching for my return."

We laughed and we hugged again and then I confessed to the brown paper bags. Inside there was an apple, an orange, a candy cane, peppermints, ribbon candy, peanuts and a small mixture of Brazil, hazelnut, almond and walnuts. What a bounty.

After we oohed and ahed over this delightful treat, Ma confessed, "I heard you take out the cloth from the drawer. I was glad you did that as I wasn't sure where to put your mittens."

Again we hugged and laughed, relishing in the wonder of surprise, in the wonder of Christmas. It was then I knew I hadn't lost the magic of Christmas. It was here at home with Ma and I loving each other and being thankful for what we had, as little as it was.

Even the despicable chicken I had to clean the day before tasted good.

CHAPTER 28

The new year came in with a blast of cold air and snow. The wind whirled the huge densely falling snowflakes around and around the house finally letting them fall to the ground, building in layers until the snow was two feet high or higher. After a few days, the snow stopped falling but the wind increased its velocity blowing all the fluffy new fallen snow into hard packed drifts.

On those days, our activities were curbed to doing the chores, keeping the fire going in the stove, and making pots of tea that we drank with our feet in the oven.

Doing the chores on those days took longer than normal. By the time I reached the barrel into which I emptied the ashes, the ash pan was not as full as when I started. The wind had blown most of the ashes all over me.

Bringing in the coal was heavy work. Carrying the two five-gallon pails and the coal pail in one hand, I plowed through the knee-deep snow, keeping close to the house. At the corner, my empty hand reached for the rope that was tied at the other end to the coal shed. With the wind buffeting me from all directions—or so it seemed—I finally reached the coal shed where I filled the three pails full of coal. Three trips to the house completed that mission.

Then there were numerous trips to the house with armfuls of wood taken from the same shed.

Taking Ma to the out house was at least a half hour excursion. Outside clothing was donned, and as we went out the door, I picked up a few of the newspaper squares I had cut for outhouse purposes.

Taking Ma by the hand, my other hand guided us along the house, the rope to the shed, past the shed, and then onto another rope that took us to our facility. Because it was a small building, I waited for Ma outside, trying to keep out of the wind.

Upon returning to the house and her rocking chair by the stove, Ma's heavy breathing was interrupted by spasmodic coughing. I was glad those excursions didn't happen too often during the day.

Once the storm had blown over, the sun shone brightly but cold. Everything looked so white and clean. Chores were much easier especially after I got the idea to use the sled.

Two pails of coal made the runners sink somewhat into the snow. Even then, pulling was still easier than carrying. I was able to put a couple of armfuls of wood on the sled, cutting my trips with wood in half.

After using it the first time, I hung it in the coal/wood shed with the runners outward. In the process, I noticed some writing on the underside of the wood. On closer examination I read, "To Pe...r From M..her an. .the."

This WAS Peter's sled. And indescribable warmth crept through me. Beautiful memories flooded my brain. Not only when I was with them, but stories that Olga would relate to me about how much fun they were having with Peter's sled.

Taking my mittens off, I lovingly touched the runners, the wood, and the writing. Peter was still with me.

I didn't want to return to the house. The sun, although not shedding much warmth, was bright and cheerful. My heart felt the same way.

Leaving the shed, I looked around wondering what to do and where to go. I headed for the north side of the barn where Peter had first called me his 'Lady Godiva'. Our 'love nest' was too far away. A storm could come up anytime.

I wandered around the yard, all the while walking on the top of the hard wind-blown snowdrifts. It was like playing 'King of the Castle'. When I broke through the crust sinking to my knees or deeper, I laughed for joy, not minding the snow that fell into my overshoes to melt and make my feet cold. It felt so good to be a kid again.

Even though I was beginning to feel chilled, I still didn't want to go inside. It was so bright, unlike the days when the snowstorm dimmed the daylight. I knew I had to resist the temptation to stay out longer as I remembered our ice-making escapade and how sick I was after. I couldn't afford to get sick as Ma depended on my too much.

Around the first of February, 1942, I had the opportunity to go to town again. I was excited, remembering the previous trip. I gave Ma the same instructions, made another good-tasking cheese sandwich, took hold of the frayed braided twine of the sled, and set off with a glad heart. I promised Ma I would be home before dark and vowed to myself this time I would not break that promise.

I knew the town wouldn't be quite the same. The tree would be gone along with other Christmas decorations including the animated elves. But I was disappointed in the change of the people.

En route to the post office, I met a few people who looked neither left nor right nor even smiled as they went on their way, their minds focused on what they had to do.

The postmistress, however, had a cheerful smile as she handed me a letter saying, "I imagine you'll be glad to get this. It came the day after you came in. Too bad you couldn't have had it to read on Christmas Day."

The letter gave me joy, but her remark hurt. She didn't know how I suffered through Christmas and the snowstorm without a new letter from Peter.

I left the post office and headed for Mr. Black's grocery store. First, I made a stop at the thrift shop. That lady was so pleasant I thought I would say 'hello'.

When I entered, the lady came forward pleasantly saying, "Good afternoon, Miss. May I help you?"

"Oh, ah, yes, no," I stammered. "I just dropped in to say how glad I am to have the sled I bought from you at Christmas."

"Oh, yes. I remember now. Is everything alright?"

"Yes, Madam. And Ma likes her brooch too."

"I have some more pieces from that same lady. Would you like to see them?"

"Thank you, no. I just came in to say hello and to tell you how pleased we are with our purchases."

"Well, thank you. I have some paper work I must do so if you'll just excuse me."

"Sorry to have kept you from your work," I apologized.

"Not at all. Nice to see you. Bye for now," and she left me to make my way out alone.

"If that is what they call a cold shoulder, I guess I've had it," I thought as I crossed the street to Mr. Black's.

Mr. Black, however, was glad to see me. His greeting was warm and sincere as he shook hands with me and asked about Ma.

When my few purchases were all bundled up, Mr. Black asked, "Are you walking?"

"Yes, I am. I saved the twine from last time so I can tie my bundles on the sled."

"Here, let me help you," Mr. Black said as he took his jacket from the peg by the door.

Soon I was on my way with Mr. Black's well wishes echoing in my heart and mind.

The trek home was uneventful. No choir singing and no coyotes. And I was home by 3:300 in the afternoon.

"How can people change so fast?" I asked Ma after I told her of my brush with humanity.

Ellen's Story

"I don't know, Ellen," she said slowly. "I don't know.

CHAPTER 29

No matter what the personalities of the town folk were like, we still needed some supplies. The weekly newspapers that dear Mr. Black saved for me, were the most precious items. Some of the news was two to three weeks old, depending how frequent were my trips, but it kept us in contact with the world, especially the war.

Peter's letters were few and far between, some hasty little notes letting us know he was still alive, some telling tales of a night out on the town with the guys. At first, I had a hard time accepting the fact that Peter would drink so much alcohol that he would become drunk. They say that a great deal of alcohol helps you to forget. But once you get it out of your system, isn't the real world just the same? I guess that is one aspect of life I will never understand.

Periodically, as I reached the town, there would be a huge noisy crowd of people all reaching with eager hands for the pieces of paper that the telegraph operator was handing out his window of the railway station's telegraph office. These papers had names of the local men and women who had lost their lives in the battle of a few days earlier. Tom and Mr. DeJong were always there. I would watch their faces while they scanned the page for Peter's name. When they smiled, I knew all was well. Sometimes they would see me and call out, "Hello, Ellen. I guess we can smile a while yet." Then off they would go, my heart replacing itself in my chest.

Then I would look at others. Some were glad like us but others wept—a man tried to console his wife as she repeatedly beat on his chest while shouting, "No. No. No." A young woman with a small child tugging at her skirt stared into space; an old man sat on the bench letting his tears fall freely. I couldn't help but join Ma in her prayers on those evenings.

Ellen's Story

The problems of the town and the world seemed to be so far away as Ma and I led our hum-drum life–breakfast, sweep floor, take care of the stove, knit socks, read and re-read newspapers and Peter's letters, supper, dishes, meditation, and bedtime.

In that spring of 1942, an event happened that bothered me for many years. I couldn't tell Ma about it as she would not have been able to help me anyway. I couldn't tell Olga; she wasn't around. If she had been at home, the embarrassing incident would not have happened.

It was a beautiful spring day in May. I decided to plant a few seeds of vegetables and some flowers. It would keep me busy, give us fresh food, and something pretty to look at.

I went out about mid-morning to the old house where we once lived to get a spade. We used the old house to store garden tools as it was so close to the garden spot. I picked out the short handled one as it would be easier to handle.

I wasn't going to dig up the whole garden. That would have been far too much work and far too much for us to eat. It wasn't an easy task. The ground on the prairies packs hard with the wind blowing away the best of the topsoil. Periodically, I had to stop and straighten up, viewing my accomplishment as I did so.

I was getting quite a bit done even though I was getting hot from work and the sun. The ever-present breeze, however, had a cooling effect as it blew my skirt up and around my bare legs. I didn't mind my legs showing. There was only Ma and me there and being we lived at the end of the road, which I had my back to, there was no passing traffic.

I finally decided to leave the digging. I needed a break for food, water, rest, and to decide whether or not my little plot was big enough.

Dianne Osborne

Pushing the spade into the ground with my foot, I left it there, standing on its own. "I'll put it away later if I don't need it," was a fleeting thought on my mind. Pleased and content with myself, I turned to head for the house and froze. My heart leaped into my mouth causing it to gape open, and my eyes grew round and wide open. About thirty feet away stood Olga's husband, Tom.

He was running his thick tongue over his full, pouty lips with his eyes focused on my legs. When he realized that he was looking at the front instead of the back, he looked into my face with lustful eyes and said, "You have nice legs, Ellen. It's been a long time since I've seen a pair of bare legs."

Suddenly, I wanted to vomit. This fat slobbering 'pig'–I could never understand what Olga saw in him–was blatantly admiring my body in a way that was sickening right down to my very soul. I understood he was a young man and that his equally young wife had been in the sanitarium for over six months, but, for God's sake, have some control.

I couldn't speak. I couldn't move. I couldn't think.

He started to make a move towards me with his arms outstretched. "Give me a kiss, Ellen. Just a little one. I really need one."

His action moved my brain and my mouth. Between clenched teeth and above a vibrantly beating frightened heart, I hissed out, "Don't you DARE take one step closer. Turn around and get your fat ass out of here and don't ever come back."

He stopped but made no attempt to carry out my orders. "Please," he begged.

"I'm warning you, Tom!" I reached for the spade.

After a moment, he shrugged his shoulders and then unhurriedly turned around. Slowly, he put one foot before the other until he was gone from our lane, down the road and out of my sight.

142

Ellen's Story

My body relaxed and became jelly. I slumped to the ground, letting all the air out of my lungs that I had subconsciously been holding in. My stomach churned and tears rolled down my cheeks. I felt so humiliated I wanted to die. Never again will I be able to face Olga or her father without this incident coming to mind. I didn't know at that time that that was the beginning of the end of our friendship.

After awhile, enough strength came back to me to get me to the house. Maybe a drink of water will help settle my stomach.

When I entered, Ma called from the living room, "Was that Tom I saw passing the window?"

"Yes, Ma. It was," I said in a dead voice.

"What did he want? He looked so forlorn. Poor fellow, so young and having to live alone. He looked as if you didn't cheer him up very much."

"No, Ma, I didn't."

"Oh, well. We all have our problems." She went back to whatever she was doing.

CHAPTER 30

The incident had a great effect on my gardening. I had become quite enthused before it happened about doing the work and the rewards. After Tom's visit, I would scrutinize the road when I went to the garden to make sure Tom wasn't coming back. As I hoed and weeded, the breeze and wind would bare my legs to the world. Many times I would suddenly stop what I was doing and whirl around fast as if to catch someone watching me. Tom never did come back. I was glad in a sort of way when winter came causing the garden work to stop. I knew time would heal. Hopefully by next spring, I would feel free again to joyfully put in another garden.

I did, however, have a bit of a scare one day in the fall when I saw someone walking up the road. It turned out to be Mr. DeJong enquiring if we would need coal and that he would bring it.

I went with him the day he went for coal and bought as much flour, sugar, and other staples that our ration books would allow us to buy. The garden would sustain us. What other little things we might need I could carry home or pull on Peter's sled. There would be no baubles for Ma this Christmas. My savings would be gone by spring. What I would do then I didn't know. I had all winter to think about it.

And so the winter set in—the blizzards, the bright sun and full moon on freshly fallen snow, 'King of the Castle' snow banks, crisp days, and dreary days. Sometimes my trips were real quick ones. Although the sky was clear in the morning, it was clouding in dark and fast by noontime. "Hello, good-bye, and thank you for the newspaper" to the Blacks, and I was off for home in a hurry. Sometimes I would get there in time. Other times I had to follow the light Ma always put in the window. I would be like a snowman by the time I walked through the door.

Ellen's Story

Spring came, and with it my financial problem. I had no problem walking to town now but where would I work. Employees were making just enough for themselves.

Surprisingly and yet not so surprisingly, our answer came from Mr. DeJong.

He came riding up our lane one balmy late April afternoon in 1943 on his horse. He was quite cheerful. No doubt, like us, he was glad the winter was over.

"Good afternoon, Ellen," he greeted me as I stepped out the door to meet him.

"And a good afternoon to you, too, Mr. DeJong." Odd how cheerfulness can be so infectious. "What can I do for you?"

"Well, Ellen. It's like this. Young Mrs. Beaverly just east of me lost her husband. Unfortunately his name was on the list. She is alone, no children, which I guess we can say is a blessing."

I nodded in agreement.

"Anyway, she had a few head of cattle and asked me if I could buy them from her. Well, now, I don't have much money I told her.

"Oh, just enough to get me to the city. I have a sister there," she said.

"So we shook hands and that was that. But now I am going to need more hay and I was wondering if I could buy your hay. Tom and I would do the work. I can't pay much but I could buy your coal for you, bring you some chickens, or whatever, and maybe, depending on the market, a little bit of cash."

The mention of Tom gave me a shiver but the chickenS brought to mind our Christmas a year ago so I said, "I would love to have the chickens but they have to be cleaned."

He frowned not knowing what I was getting at. So I related the story of finding the plucked chicken in the porch and how I had never cleaned a chicken before. We had a good laugh over that.

145

Dianne Osborne

So the deal was sealed once again as with Mrs. Beaverly, with a handshake. I felt good inside, believing maybe I can forgive and forget. Of course, I didn't know what the future would bring.

The future brought Olga home that fall as a frail and pale complexioned specimen of a once joyful and fun-loving girl. She still had an infectious laugh that made everyone around her glad to be in her presence. It had thinned out, however, both in volume and frequency.

That first afternoon we had together was at her father's farm, an easy distance for me to walk. It was a joy to see her again, but for me it was also a strain and yet a relief. Tom never looked at me unless it was necessary. I continued to wonder what Olga found so wonderful about him but said nothing. It was none of my business. My laughs during the afternoon were too spontaneous. Anyone knowing the story would class them as laughs of relief.

During the course of the winter, I visited infrequently as it tired her so much. Besides our relationship was not the same. I still liked her. I still felt she would be my future sister-in-law. But it just wasn't the same.

CHAPTER 31

It was getting close to the spring of 1944. So much had happened in the war, so many lost battles, so many lost lives, and so much low moral. Winston Churchill's words of encouragement were a comfort to so many. Now that the tide of events seemed to be turning for the allies, people began to hope once again.

My hopes didn't gain any new heights after reading the following long letter from Peter. He wrote very few words of preliminary greetings. He had too long of a story to tell.

"...*proud and glad to be called upon as one of four guys to do this particular job. There wasn't much time between the decision to demolish the fuel depot and the actual performing of the duty. We studied maps, diagrams and procedures for hours then were briefed on the danger of the job, the chance of survival and what to do if we did survive. When all was learned we were asked if we still were willing to go ahead with it. All of us gave the thumbs up signal.*

The depot was a four story circular structure of stone and cement about five miles from a village. It was built on a flat piece of land with a cliff behind it. Each floor was compactly storing barrels of fuel. To walk into the main door to lay our fuses would have been suicidal as it was well guarded by at least a dozen German soldiers. However, fortunately for us there was a door on the top floor and a balcony all around. A pointed turret like roof topped this edifice.

To gain access to this building unnoticed would have to be through the door in the top floor which was fifty to sixty feet from the top of the cliff. We did the impossible. We reached the top floor balcony via a rope.

We wrapped a grappling hook around and around with yards of cloth to make it padded. Standing at the edge of the cliff, we swung the rope attached to the hook and holding our breaths while it sailed through the air to land on the balcony railing with a thud. Giving a tug to secure it we tightened the rope and tied it to a nearby huge tree. Then we waited a few seconds for any repercussion.

147

Dianne Osborne

Hearing only silence each one of us took our turn going hand over hand on the rope stretched taught thirty to forty feet in the air until each one of us landed safely on the balcony.

There was a gliche to this expedition. There was a German sentry patrolling the circumference of the building. Slowly he walked with rifle in hand and eyes looking everywhere as he made his rounds. As soon as he was out of sight, a man made his trip across the rope immediately flattening himself against the wall. The sentry would pass below. Then another would cross. A quick pick of the lock and we were inside.

Each fourteen to sixteen foot in diameter room was filled to near capacity with barrels of fuel. We lit our fuses with each of us taking turns on each floor as lookout man. On each floor the fuses had to be lit for a different time space so that all fuses ignited at the same time.

Descending the last set of stairs that led to an office of some kind was done with beating heart and silent foot. By this time, because of the lack of windows, we were not sure where the German sentry was as he made his rounds.

We were about to set foot into this office when the sentry came in. Our minds travelled to the fuses we had just lit which were to go off simultaneously and in any second from now. A split decision had to be made to save our own lives. Only one of us was armed. Could he get both of them before one of them got one of us?

Suddenly the sentry was gone. We made our move into the room. The armed man's pistol arm aimed at the officer at the desk. The officer shouted. Our man fired. The sentry re-entered. Again our man fired. We scrambled over the dead bodies out the door and headed for the hills that lay near the flat ground of the yard.

Not knowing where the enemy was at the fuel depot we ran zigzag fashion, crouching low. Suddenly I was hit with a blow from behind. L.P."

"Oh!" I said as I let out my breath.

There was no more letter. Peter had used up every inch of his paper. In order to get everything in he wrote very small. He couldn't sigh off in his usual way. There was hardly any room left for the "L. P."–"Love, Peter".

I sat for a long time holding his letter, staring at his writing, just thinking. Peter was a witness to the killing of two men. "Yes, Ellen," I reasoned with myself, "that is what happens in wars. No doubt he had witnessed many killings, maybe killed a few himself."

What kind of a person will Peter be like when he comes home? Death, cigarettes, and alcohol–his chatty letters told of good times in the pubs drinking too much wine–will all have a marked affect on his life. Or would it? Will he be able to stop smoking and drinking and put death behind him becoming once again the kind, loving, gentle Peter of old?

The killing of the two men bothered me for some days. Reading about so many people killed in such and such a battle didn't have the same effect. Maybe because Peter was so close to my heart in comparison to the generality of the newspaper reports.

But what happened to Peter? He was still alive evidenced by him writing his letter. But was he now alive? This letter was written weeks ago. Was he taken prisoner? Was he being mistreated? Tortured? It was hard for me to settle down to the caring of Ma, the house and the garden.

CHAPTER 32

The days were beginning to get quite warm and so was my upstairs bedroom. The combination of warm nights and Peter's letter caused me many sleepless nights. I was thankful that Ma slept downstairs where it was cooler. This helped her to have relatively good night rests with only the occasional coughing spell.

Then came the warm night of restless sleep for Ma and me too. I could hear her coughing almost continually. Her old bed did a great deal of squeaking as she tossed her heavy body from side to side. Then somewhere near early morning all was quiet from her night quarters. I was relieved that sleep had finally come for her enabling her to rest peacefully. Relaxing, I, too, slept for some time.

It was well into the morning when I finally rose, dressed, and made my way down to the kitchen to make a light breakfast for us.

I went to Ma to see if she would be satisfied with bread and jam rather than toast and jam. It took too long to get the coals in the stove just right for toast. By that time the house would be too warm.

As I neared her, I could see that her thin sheet had really entangled her as she tossed and turned. And then I saw her face..

It had become quite swollen out of shape, turning to a bluish color. Her eyes were wide open staring at the ceiling. Blood trickled out of the corner of her gaping mouth.

I think I screamed. I don't know. I don't know how I got to town. My focus was getting help from Mr. Black, my new found and wonderful friend. I didn't know what kind of help I would need; I just knew I needed help.

After Mr. And Mrs. Black deciphered my gibberish, a doctor was called who took me home where the DeJongs came soon after seeing the doctor's car go by going at least 30 mph.

Ellen's Story

The doctor examined Ma–at least he took one or two looks at her–pronounced her dead and filled out a sheet of paper. He then came to me putting both my hands between his two kind gentle hands. Looking straight into my face, he said, "Ellen, you are in shock. Seeing a dead person, especially a loved one is bad enough. Your Ma's appearance is worse than an ordinary death. I am going to give you a needle to help calm you. Do you have somewhere to go to for at least this one night?"

I shook my head, but Olga quickly stepped in saying, "She can come to our house. Many times before when there has been sickness here she has come home to us."

"Thank you, Olga," said the doctor. "Is that okay with you, Ellen?"

I just shrugged my shoulders. "I guess so," I whispered.

As Olga took my arm to lead me out of the house, I turned to look at Ma.

"We'll take care of her," the doctor reassured me.

Olga put me in Peter's room as she and Tom shared her old room. I sat numbly on the side of the bed, looking around at Peter's things from childhood to adolescence. I thought of Peter's letter. Did some of the dead people he saw look like Ma? Or were some like Pa, resembling a sleeping person? I began to understand why he smoked a cigarette or drank a glass or two of wine.

"Oh, Peter. I'll be so glad to have you home again, to care for you, to love you, to help you as we farm Pa's land."

Just being close to Peter's things and thinking of him comforted me, and I spent a fairly comfortable night.

I was up early as were the others. We silently ate a huge breakfast of homegrown and cured ham, farm eggs, hash browns and homemade bread toast washed down with weak coffee–coffee was expensive. I should say they ate a huge breakfast. I knew I should eat for strength, but I just couldn't get too much food down my throat.

As we finished, Mr. DeJong took my hand and gently said, "Ellen, this is a very sad and hard time for you. We've always been here to help you, your Pa, and your Ma, and we would be glad to do it again. The doctor and I made some plans yesterday, but we can't go ahead without your permission."

I had made decisions before many times on my own but yet not alone. Now I had no family, other than the DeJongs who had once again come to my rescue, to help me decide what was to be done. I was entirely on my own. I asked, "What were the plans?"

"A few neighbours are willing to dig the grave beside your Pa's as well as make a coffin out of the old barn boards. The doctor has agreed to look after your Ma's body. We could have the funeral around 2 o'clock this afternoon. Tom could say a few words like he did at your Pa's funeral and that would be that."

That is what happened. After everyone left, I made a wooden cross from the boards and with a crayon wrote "MA" on the horizontal arm of the cross to match the cross at Pa's grave site.

The neighbours were also good enough to take Ma's bed out to one of the sheds. Also they burned the mattress, which was the doctor's order. I swept and washed the floor where her bed was and took her clothes upstairs to her old room. Pushing Pa's old couch back a little gave me some room.

When all was tidy, I went out to the bench on the south side of the shed that once was our home. I sat there looking out over the garden, the grey soil showing rows of new green sprouts of vegetables and flowers.

The sun set over the prairies in a glow of pinks and purples. The air was still and peaceful. The odd bird was heard and a lowing of a cow at the neighbours. Otherwise all was quiet. The serenity of the atmosphere comforted me. Ma and Pa were at last together. Later, no doubt much later, I would join them. But first Peter and I would farm and raise a family right here on this land that was now totally mine.

CHAPTER 33

And so I started a new life—well, in a way. I cared for the garden, the house, and made biweekly trips to town to pick up the newspapers from Mr. Black and look for some news from Peter.

For the most part, the days were sunny with an odd shower or two. During an exceptionally long rainy spell, I tired of re-reading the newspapers, Peter's letters, and knitting socks. I became restless. I sat on Pa's old couch watching the rain wash the windows and thought of Ma, of how she sat for days just watching the windows. Then she would write in her journal and read a scripture or two.

But what did she write since she never did anything? Maybe she wrote her thoughts down. I thought about that concept for a while, coming to the conclusion that it was a good idea to start my own journal. I don't do much, but I certainly think a great deal.

I went to the buffet drawer to see if there was some writing paper there to start a journal of my own. Her Bible blinked up at me as I pulled the drawer open. I picked it up. Rippling the pages, I noticed many passages underlined and some notes on the side of the page.

Directly below where the Bible had lain was her diary or should I say diaries. When she left Ireland, her family had given her a proper diary book. When I started school, she saved my old scribblers to write in her small penmanship, above each line of my writing. As finances got worse she used the brown paper bags. She cried with glee one Christmas many years back when she received writing paper from our family across the pond. When the paper was used up she carefully opened the envelopes to write on both side. Her latest entries were on brown paper bags.

Everything was dated carefully with all in order. I looked at them a long time before carefully lifting them from the drawer. To read these would help me understand many things I wondered about.

But, I argued, this is someone else's private life and thoughts. Isn't it a nosy person who delves into someone else's business? But this is Ma's, my mother's, and my flesh and blood. So much could be benefited—maybe—by reading her history and probably mine too.

I took the book from Ireland from its resting place. It looked as if it hadn't been opened in years. I took it to Pa's couch, holding it on my lap for a long time. Finally, I opened the cover. On the flyleaf was written, "To Catherine, have a safe journey. Love Aunt Colleen and Uncle Oliver. Feb. 1925."

I started reading under the first date of Feb. 25, 1925. As I read the daily entries, I was able to get the picture of the excitement, joy, and sadness of these three families—Ma, Pa and me and Ma's family and Pa's family—parting, knowing that they probably would never see each other again.

Pa had been given his inheritance money from his father. This money was to be used for passage to Canada and the purchase of land with livestock and machinery being bought with whatever was left. Ma told of our train journey from County Tyrone in the north to Cork on the south shore where we would board ship to cross the ocean.

We had to wait some days in Cork as we arrived ahead of shipping time. According to Ma, Pa was overly excited as well as being restless. She writes, "Kelly is so restless. He paced the floor of the boarding house until I thought we would have to buy the landlord a new carpet. Finally he came to me and kindly, almost begging, said, "Katie, me love, I am a very thirsty man. I would dearly love to have a pint. Would you allow me to go for one—just one—at the pub a few streets down?" I let him go. Maybe he would be in a better mood on the morrow."

He came home quite late, drunk but happy. "Katie, me love, I am the happiest man in the world," he said in his booming voice. I had to remind him to be quieter as there were other families sleeping here waiting for their passages. He didn't seem to hear for he continued, "I have a wonderful wife, the cutest daughter this side of heaven as well as having a whole lot more money than what I started with." Stupefied I asked, "What do you mean?"

"Katie, me love. It just so happens that the pub was close to the horse race track. A few were going there and they asked me along. Well, you know me. I can't go the races without betting. I bet on a bay to come in first and I bet on a long shot. The bay lost but the long-shot came in first. I doubled my money."

"How much did you bet?"

"Our passage across the sea."

"You did what?" This time it was me shouting and had to be quieted down.

"Hey, Katie, me love. Don't get so upset. I won."

"But what if you had lost?"

"But I didn't. Why worry about something that didn't happen?"

He had a point there. I shuddered, though, to think what would have become of us if he had lost.

"Oh, by the way, Katie. We're to get up early in the morning. We have to be aboard ship by noon tomorrow."

"Oh, Kelly. That is wonderful." I hugged him and kissed him and loved him all over again."

I lowered the book to my lap, my arms too weak to hold it any longer. I stared at Ma's writing, at his words, at her words. I could not believe my eyes.

"Oh, Pa." I breathed out loud. "How could you have done such a thing?"

CHAPTER 34

How long I sat there is hard to say. Finally, I became aware of my surroundings and the thoughts that had led me to the buffet drawer.

I put everything back as it was. For days, I mechanically did what had to be done, my mind full of disbelief that Pa would gamble and drink to the point of drunkenness. I wasn't sure if I wanted to read any more of Ma's diaries. I wasn't sure if I wanted my ideal vision of what I thought Pa was–kind, fun-loving, caring–to be distorted, if indeed there were other incidents that would show his other side.

Summer waned, turning to autumn. I mostly burned coal for heat and cooking, but some wood had to be burned to get a good fire started. I would find the wood in the ravine's bushes bringing it home tied with twine to Peter's sled. It was hard pulling on the dirt, but not so bad on the grass. I had to go a little farther down the ravine each year to bring the dead branches home. This took a great deal of time. No matter, time was what I had plenty of. Some of the sheds and part of the barn were starting to fall apart. By cleaning the old boards up and putting them into the woodshed with the branches, it cleaned the yard as well as supplying me with kindling and cooking fuel.

It was nearing the end of October when Mr. DeJong came for me with his wagon. I didn't need many other supplies; the garden yielded well again. It was just a joy to ride to town instead of walk.

That evening, I sat on Pa's old couch with a feeling of contentment. Let the winds blow and the snow fly. I would eat and be able to keep warm. I had some new newspapers to be read but most joyful of all was a letter from Peter. He was alive. In what condition I didn't know until I read the letter. The main thing was that he was alive.

With eager shaking fingers I opened his letter—another long one in tiny handwriting. It went like this:

"My face and body hit the ground all at the same time knocking the wind out of me, possibly loosing consciousness for a few seconds. I was aware of a great roar behind me coupled with a huge flickering light. Instinctively I knew that the depot had blown, the force of the blast driving me to the ground. Adrenalin pumped through my veins driving me to stand and run again and not to stop till I was well away from the area.

I didn't see the other fellows. Orders were to take care of yourself and only yourself. When my chest was bursting from lack of air, I slowed to a fast walk then turned to see the results of our efforts. Being that the depot was in a valley and I had traveled up and over a few hills, only a huge flickering orange and yellow glow in the sky was seen. Being night the black smoke was barely visible.

When the reports of the incident were brought forth later, we found that most of the windows in the village had been blown out and some of the older buildings had collapsed from the force of the explosion.

Tired as I was I had to keep going using the night sky for cover. Towards dawn I found a culvert to crawl into to rest as best I could during the daylight hours.

I stayed awake for a while but it wasn't long before weariness and relaxed nerves—the job had been a success—caused me to doze only to be awakened— God knows how long after—by the sound of harsh German orders and marching feet.

The culvert was only approximately three feet in diameter with dirty, leaf infested water running through it. To avoid getting wet I sat on one side of the water, my feet on the other side allowing the water to trickle beneath my raised knees. My knees with arms folded on them gave me my pillow as I dozed and tried to rest.

I must have slept a fair while before hearing the enemy approach as my neck and shoulders were beginning to ache due to the cramped position I was in. Discomfort was pushed aside as I began to wonder what the German soldier had said. Was he an officer ordering his troop to look into any small opening or shelter for the culprits responsible for the demolishing of the depot? Were they told to shoot and ask questions later?

I couldn't run from my hiding place, as the field was too open making me a visible target. To stay was also dangerous.

I decided to stay. As they came closer I held my breath and closed my eyes knowing it wasn't really going to help my situation but I felt better.

The marching feet came closer. No one spoke. Closer and closer. Then they were overhead making the ground vibrate. As heavy footsteps faded away I was relieved that I had survived my first encounter with danger. Hopefully it would set the precedent for other dangers. I was still a long way from the reporting officer at the barracks.

Just as darkness was setting in I cautiously and with great difficulty crawled from my hiding place. Sitting in a cramped position all day with only the capability of flexing a few muscles from time to time caused some concern as to how well my legs were going to work.

I made a dash as quick, as my stiff body would allow me, to a nearby bush. Here I did some quick exercises then checked my bearings with my compass. According to the compass and the memory of the map I had studied I was to head towards the mountain standing at a mile or so in the distance. Once there I would find a path that led up the side, leveled out then descended later into a village where I would speak a password, eventually finding my contact person. He would contact barracks then show me the safest way back.

There was no moon but plenty of stars. The darkness was a blessing but once on the well-vegetated path it slowed me down. As dawn was breaking, my solitary thoughts were broken my sounds of voices. I stopped. I listened. No, they weren't Germans. Carefully and in a crouched position I continued using the grass by the path to silence my own footfalls. Rounding a bend I saw them but, to my dismay, I stepped on a twig at the same time. Of course, it made a loud snap. The voices stopped immediately. Slowly they turned to look in the direction of the noise. I hoped I was crouched low enough for the bush to hide me. Eventually they turned back to themselves, made some low mutterings and continued on their way after hefting large grain bags to the top of the heads.

They gave the appearance of peasants going to market with their grain. The long black hair of the two women hung in a single braid down their back. Shawls covering their shoulders were slid to their heads when they carried the grain on their heads. Long colorful voluminous skirts had aprons protecting the fronts of the skirts. The three men wore long jerkin type vests over long, puffed sleeved tunics. Their black baggy pants met the top of their sandals worn over bare feet. Small caps protected their heads and hair from the grain dust of the sacks.

I waited a few minutes then completely rounded the bend to observe whatever I could. They were still walking away from me but soon stopped, putting their sacks to the ground with ease.

Daylight was creeping in quite fast but I waited a moment longer. They pulled their sacks into the bush. The women produced bread and cheese from their big apron pockets. After eating quietly they too disappeared from sight, no doubt making themselves a "bed" for the day.

Having seen enough to satisfy my curiosity I crept back some hundred feet or so and made my own bed. The sight of the food made me realize how hungry I was. But a gnawing stomach didn't bother me as much as the five people ahead of me.

I came to the conclusion that they were not peasants but part of smugglers. Farmers would travel by day and sleep by night as they had nothing to hide. No doubt, drugs or weapons or both were nestled in the grain they carried on their heads. Where were they taking it to—the enemy, the allies or their own people? Wherever, I couldn't let them know of my presence.

For three more days and nights we traveled "together", keeping a fair distance between us. If I got too close I could hear the rustle of their clothing and five sets of footsteps so I would slow down.

The last morning on the mountainside brought a grey chilling dawn. Heavy clouds filled the sky threatening rain or maybe even snow, it was so cold. I went further off the path then usual looking for a big spruce tree to lie under. They were spindly so I chose the best one curling up trying to cover myself with dried leaves and such. I didn't want to sleep too soundly—there was more danger than just my "companions"—but fatigue got the best of me and I slept like a baby. A warm cozy feeling woke me. Becoming slowly aware of my surrounding I realized I was covered in a blanket of snow with flakes still coming down.

Although comforting it posed another problem—my tracks could be readily seen unless it continued to snow all night.

Darkness fell and I crawled out from under my blanket. The others were well ahead of me. As we traveled we started to descend the mountain, viewing the village from time to time through the branches of the trees as they became more sparse. The path turned to mud and the flakes of snow to drops of rain. By dawn we were at the edge of the shelter of trees. They bedded down and so did I.

That evening they entered the village in the late afternoon walking boldly as if indeed they were peasants. I waited till almost midnight before following the village map I kept in my mind's eye to a humble little cottage. Here I knocked and whispered the password.

It took a few seconds before the door opened as the occupants inside first had to blow out the candle. Even so the door opened only wide enough for me to squeeze in. A few formal words of code passed before I was welcomed into the allies" arms. L. P."

What a relief. Peter is alive and relatively well. But wait. What was the date on the letter? February 1944. Ortona was December 1943, wasn't it? According to the newspaper it was a real battle for the Canadians. Did he take part in it? Was this part of their victory? So many questions. How long would I have to wait for answers?

I sighed. What to do? I took a look at my surroundings. Although not much to look at, I had at least warmth, shelter, and food everyday. The best thing I could do was to be thankful for that and to keep myself whole and healthy so that when Peter came back I could be help to him.

161

CHAPTER 35

When the first snowfall came that fall of 1944, I didn't mind the thought that my outdoor activities would now be curtailed. The knowledge that Peter was alive–his letter verified that and his family (who would be the first to know) hadn't told me otherwise– gave me a contented feeling.

I slipped into winter with ease, getting into my winter chore schedule with knitting more socks to fill in the rest of my time.

I made a trip to town shortly before Christmas. The tree was standing alone in the intersection. 'Santa Claus' wouldn't arrive till later. I treated myself to some ribbon candy, nuts, and oranges to take home with my newspapers. Rarely did I get mail, only from Peter. His letters were far and few between. I left town early with special seasons greetings from Mr. And Mrs. Black ringing in my ears.

Christmas morning, I ate one of the two oranges before my toast and tea. The whole day stretched ahead of me after chores were done. What to do? I didn't want to knit socks. This was a special day, and I wanted to have a special day, too. But how?

I went into the living room just after lunch seeking pleasure. Near the buffet, I stopped and unconsciously put my hand on it. I noticed the books across the room on the apple box shelves. They didn't quite appeal to me. Reading newspapers and old magazines from days way back when was 'old hat'. I wanted something new.

Sighing, I turned to go and saw my hand on the buffet. The diaries. No, I can't. It was too disturbing. But that was only one incident. Surely Pa didn't do wrong once he arrived here. I don't remember anything about him except his hearty laugh and his joy at being in Canada. Of course, the heartbreak was there, but that was due to the depression and sickness. Wasn't it?

Ellen's Story

I slowly drew the drawer open. Everything was as I left it. I took the books to Pa's old couch that I had covered with a couple of blankets to make it somewhat more comfortable and sat down. I reached for the book, the first of the diaries, and opened it to the page where I had left off.

I skimmed across the pages, as most of it was just every day occurrences. Ma did say how excited she was at meeting the neighbours and how glad she was her little girl would have playmates so close by.

I came to the time when Pa went to town by himself, and Ma was so disappointed she couldn't go too. I reread that as I remembered it well, how Pa was so jubilant when he came home. Ma wrote, "When he gave me a good-night kiss I could smell the whiskey on his breath but I said nothing. I felt he deserved a couple of drinks. I knew he didn't get drunk today; he didn't have the time. Besides the cold trip home would have sobered him."

I had to agree with Ma now that I'm older and understand so much more. I read on until Ma's fall by the well that Pa was digging. I was shocked to find that the cause of her sickness was a miscarriage. She never said anything about it when we chatted in the evenings. Maybe it was too sad for her to talk about.

I was doubly shocked to read the reason for my second stay at the DeJongs the following summer was another miscarriage.

I stopped reading for a while. How different things might be now. I would have two siblings to care for. One would be eighteen and maybe off to war by now, the other seventeen, maybe lying about his age and gone too. That is if they had been the sons Pa looked anxiously forward to. If they had been girls, what fun we could be having, chatting and dreaming while we knit socks for the soldiers. I read on.

I came to the day when Andrew brought me home from school just in time to see Pa rush from the house with a bundle of cloth that needed to be buried. This caused a rather lengthy stay for me at the DeJongs much to my bewilderment. Ma's handwriting that lay on my lap finally answered the reason for Pa's haloed ground.

She wrote: "Zelda caught me crying. She sat on the side of my bed quietly holding my hand, letting my tears take their course. Finally I whispered, "Why did it have to be a boy?"

"Would it not have been as bad if it was a girl?" Zelda gently asked me.

I had to admit I would still feel this sadness, this emptiness, and this failure. "No, it's just that Kelly had wanted a son for so long. I won't blame him if he goes on a three day drunk. I almost feel like joining him." Then I burst into tears again.

"Oh. Oh. Oh!" I cried. I jumped to my feet, the book falling to the floor. I felt a need for movement. I dashed to the porch, threw on my overshoes, coat, and scarf. I had to get to the haloed ground.

The wind had blown most of the snow away along the edge of the ravine baring my little graveyard. I stood for a second looking at Ma and Pa's crude wooden crosses. I looked long and hard at the spot beside Pa's grave that he had called haloed ground. I stared and stared as if by staring an image of my little brother would come into view.

My knees buckled throwing me near his little grave, and I cried. I didn't feel the coldness of the ground only its warmth. Here lay the missing link to our family's full scope of happiness. Someday I will lie beside Ma bringing us all together. Oddly enough, Peter didn't come into the picture. It was if he was an outsider. I didn't want him to spoil our happiness.

Reality always sets in sooner or later. Although I knew it wasn't all that late in the day, it was starting to get dark. Winter days are always short. Stiffly, I rose to my feet feeling chilled. My hands and face were red. With one more glance at the graves I headed for the house.

I put the kettle on the stove after replenishing it with some wood. I warmed some milk in a pot then poured it over a slice of my homemade bread adding sugar and cinnamon. By the time that was eaten I was able to take my cup of tea into the living room. Sitting down on the couch among all the diaries, I felt a peace come over me. I had just received the most wonderful gift a child could receive— a brother.

CHAPTER 36

I picked up the book and laid it on the rest of the diaries, leaving it open at the page I had just read that afternoon. I left everything in that array for some days. I didn't want to put my 'family' away in a drawer.

For some days my mind was full of my 'family' as I mechanically did my daily chores. Ma's heartbreak at not being able to carry a child full term and then when she did, not being able to hold it and care for it must have been devastating to both of them. No wonder Pa went to town for a few drinks of whiskey.

As I was reading, I came to the conclusion that when Pa was troubled, when things didn't go smoothly or go according to his wishes he would take to the bottle. The chimney fire was one example; the miscarriages, arguments with a neighbour were others. Ma would write: "Kelly must have had a disagreement with one of the threshing crew. He has his own idea of how threshing should be done. I have to be thankful he only had a couple of drinks." Other times she would write about Pa's troubles. "I don't know what upset Kelly today. He took off in the mid-afternoon on Marty, heading down the creek." A day later she would record, "Must not have been too big of a problem, Kelly was gone only one night." Other times: "The problem must have really upset Kelly this time. He finally came home today after being gone for three nights. Thankfully he is in a very good humor when he gets back."

I remember Pa returning, laughing, and full of energy to do something, even to the point of doing something that really wasn't very important.

If Pa drank after small problems, what did he do after the death of his only son? I picked up the book again, afraid, yet curious to find out what happened.

Ellen's Story

"I've had a feeling for days that Kelly was fighting a battle within himself. Today he made his decision. "Katie, me love, I have to go to the city. I've been able to come in contact with a friend of a friend from town. He has horses and I might be able to get a good deal on them. Maybe raise horses rather than stupid cows. At any rate, I'm going into the city to talk with him and maybe make a deal. I still have some money in the bank and the crop looks good."

"I knew his 'horse dealing' was betting on the horse races. When I protested he just simply said "Remember Cork, Katie, remember Cork."

"I did remember Cork, but I also know it doesn't always work the same way. Cork, or no Cork, there was no use protesting anyway. He has his mind set. He is going to carry his plan through."

I, too, remember him reminding Ma about Cork. Now I understood so well.

Even though the races were a success, it still spelled disaster for us as has been told.

After that there were very few drinking and gambling incidents. There was no money for any of that. I skimmed through the rest of the diaries taking almost the whole month of January of 1945 to do that. So much of it I already was able to remember myself and to understand so it became boring. However, I was glad I read them. So much was explained—Ma's obesity, Pa's moodiness, their heartbreak at not making 'good' in the new country, the haloed ground, and so much more. I felt I could cope with my own life now. When Peter and I would marry, I would be able to be a much more understanding wife.

My winter passed in much the same manner as my other winters. The snow was almost all gone by the end of April. The blue sky, warm breezes of spring, and the babbling creek beckoned me to go take a closer look at nature as it burst forth in its new life.

Dandelions were popping up all over and so were the crocuses. The frogs sang a symphony for me. I could hear them but couldn't see them.

On previous walks, the distance had never extended very far. Today I felt adventurous and wanted to see beyond my horizon.

Following the creek, I neared the spot where Peter and I came to know each other. I slowed. Should I check it out more closely? "No," I decided. It has been so long, I didn't want anything to disturb me on this beautiful sunshiny day. I hurried on past.

The creek took a bend and the banks became less steep. A nice slope for cattle or horses to walk on to get a drink of the cool, clear water rippling over the rocks. Continuing, I was coming closer to the dense clump of willows that I remembered seeing from the top of the haystack.

It was a good place for sheltering if ever someone was caught in a rainstorm or even a snowstorm. The odd spruce added to the protection.

The sun and my walking on uneven ground made me warmer than just being comfortable. A cool drink of water would revive me so I made my way down the banks to the rocky edge. Carefully, I put my face into the water to drink.

My drinking caused little ripples to form catching the rays of the sun to reflect into my eyes. I stopped drinking to trickle my fingers in the water. Again little flashes of light were produced. Upon closer examination I noticed that a piece of clear glass was embedded slightly between some small stones adding to the reflections. I retrieved the glass thinking that a deer could cut his foot on it.

I looked around wondering what I should do with it when I spotted another piece. And another piece. And then a whole lot of pieces big and small.

Ellen's Story

What is this? Who was so careless to clutter the creek bank with such dangerous litter?

I went into the grove of willows and spruce hoping to find a small but strong limb to dig a hole to bury these glass pieces. The dirt in the grove would be easier to dig in and also out of sight.

My heart sank when I reached an area well inside. There were dozens of whiskey bottles piled in a pile, some broken, some still whole, one or two with a little bit of liquid in them held in by a rusty cap on the bottle neck.

I picked one up, read the faded label that verified it was whiskey. Disgusted, disappointed, yet glad to have solved another mystery, I tossed it back on the pile. It broke exuding such a terrible aroma.

"How could anyone drink this stuff? The smell is enough to knock you over," I said to the birds twittering in the branches.

They must have agreed with me as they flew away.

All thoughts of burying the glass left my mind. I looked around picturing Pa curled up under the spruce tree. If it had turned chilly, he probably didn't notice, the whiskey giving him false warmth.

I made my way out of the grove. Marty must have enjoyed his stay what with the water, good grass, and shelter if it rained.

A few yards away, I stopped and turned around. So much went through my mind. So much past history. Pa's body was buried in the farmyard, but so much of Pa was left at the grove. I knew I would never come back again. I left the bottles as a shrine to Pa.

CHAPTER 37

April turned to May. The weather was good. I decided to start digging the garden. As I worked on this loveliest of days in May, weatherise and other wise as it turned out, I heard a car come up the road and into my lane.

It was Mr. DeJong driving and frantically waving his arm out the window. Tom sat beside him also frantically waving his arm out his window. Olga, in the back seat with their two children, was just as wild in her waving.

What in the world has gotten into them? Something drastic must have happened needing them to get somewhere in a hurry. Why else would they be using the car?

Olga jumped out of the car before it came to a full stop, running over to me and grasping my arms in her hands.

"Come with us, Ellen, come with us," she excitingly screamed, spoke, screeched. "The war is over! The war is over!"

By this time, Tom and Mr. DeJong had joined us, pulling at my arm, at my sleeve.

"Hurry, everyone is celebrating in town. Come on. Hurry!"

My legs felt weak as they helped me into the back seat of the car. My mouth felt dry from hanging open, my eyes felt like they were about to pop out of my head, and my chest hurt from the thumping my heart was giving it.

The joyful news that was brought to me put only one thought in my head. Peter will soon be home.

After a few minutes, the initial shock of the good news wore off, and my heart, although still beating for Peter, was also beating for the happiness that all was over. Excitement was settling in. Wives, mothers, sweethearts will soon be reunited with their loved ones, all would be well; we could get back to our old lives again. I could tell

Mr. DeJong was excited too. He drove at least thirty miles per hour all the way into town. I wasn't sure if his eight-year-old car was going to stay together the way it shook and rattled over the ruts the spring run-off produced.

When we reached town, a large crowd was already gathered around the railway station focusing on the telegraph office window. The telegraph operator and his assistant were handing out large posters that had only three words largely printed on them—WAR IS OVER. Everyone wanted a copy. We were no different.

Mr. DeJong parked the car, retrieved copies of the poster for each of us, which we put in the glove compartment. Getting out of the car, we were immediately enveloped in the joyful madness of relief and thanksgiving. Everyone was shaking hands with everyone. Everyone was hugging everyone. I recognized neighbours, old school chums, acquaintances, and strangers alike all exclaiming; "Isn't it wonderful." Even the lady from the second-hand store gave me a warm embrace.

Above the shouting and cheers of "Hip-hip-hooray," the church bells could barely be heard. But they were ringing, ringing gladness into the hearts and souls of everyone on the street.

As the day grew on, so did the crowd as people from the surrounding area came in to participate in the celebration of freedom. Towards supper time, the café became packed. Shelves became empty in the stores as people bought bread and cheese for a quick sandwich. By early evening, the church ladies and the Red Cross had sandwiches available to those who needed them.

Darkness began to fall, and still the revelers had no idea of going home. Ticker tape and remnants of broken balloons littered the street and sidewalks. Horns and drums usually used on New Year's Eve started to appear and be heard. Everywhere was noise and laughter. Some people laughing for the sheer joy of laughing. Others laughed due to too much whiskey and (as I found out later) moonshine.

Mr. DeJong and Tom were two of those people who were indulging. Tom and Olga's wedding came to mind, remembering Mr. DeJong's announcement that he didn't give a damn who saw him. It brought a chuckle to my throat that I couldn't help but turn it into a laugh. How good it felt.

Hearing me laugh caused Mr. DeJong to take a look at me. He smiled broadly and said, "How good it is to hear you laugh, Ellen. Here, laugh some more." He handed me a paper cup half full of amber liquid.

"What is it?" I asked even though I had an idea what it was.

"Never mind what it is. Drink it," he demanded cheerfully.

Putting the cup to my mouth, I also took a sniff. It didn't quite smell like Pa's whiskey. I took a good drink. It tasted like some kind of fruit juice. A few minutes later, I finished the rest of it.

I held on to the cup as I didn't really know what to do with it. Momentarily, Tom was pouring something from a thermos bottle into it. Another drink told me it was the same stuff. Very flavorful, easy to swallow.

I think it was around midnight when I stumbled into the house and somehow made it to Pa's couch. How comfortable it felt.

I don't really remember much about coming home. I do remember the four of us laughing a great deal. The laughter turned to shrieks of gaiety when Mr. DeJong got too close to the edge of the road. His wheels headed for the ditch. He cranked on the steering wheel causing the car to careen back onto the road on two wheels. Before he could straighten the car out we were headed for the ditch on the other side of the road. After a few more swerves, he eventually had the car going in a straight direction.

Ellen's Story

During our escapade, Olga's two children, who had been sleeping, woke due to being pitched from Olga to me and back again. They started to cry not knowing where they were or what was happening. Olga just laughed and assured them that all was well, that "Grandpa was just being a kid again." And then we all laughed some more.

It wasn't a laughing matter when the late morning sun shone on my face that lay on Pa's lumpy pillow.

I opened my eyes and closed them quickly. Afraid to open them wide again, I just slowly lifted my lids enough for me to see the way to the back house. I had to relieve my bladder and quickly.

Swinging my legs to the floor, I sat up. A million trip hammers went off in my head. I sat awhile holding my head in my hands wondering how I was going to get to the back house.

With much necessity, determination, and some staggering I overcame that problem.

Being close to noon, I thought I should be hungry. Supper of yesterday was only a couple of sandwiches and that was a long time ago.

Toast was out of the question. My head would not allow the noise of starting the stove nor would it allow me to bend over to shake out the old ashes.

I finally washed a bit of bread down with a couple of swallows of milk. I ate and did very little for the next two days.

CHAPTER 38

On the evening of the second day, I began to feel more like my normal self. I sat on the bench of the shed that was once our home. I looked at the partially dug garden spot recalling the reason for stopping my work.

Never in all my born days did I think that I would let myself get drunk. Reading in the diaries about Pa's drinking made me embarrassed that my Pa would do such a thing. Peter's letters relating his nights out on leave with some of the guys from his battalion—the English beer, the fact that Italian wine was better than the French wine—appalled me that he would get in such a state he didn't know what he was doing.

And now I did the same thing. I asked myself, "Why?" The answer came up. I had something to celebrate as did Mr. DeJong at Olga's wedding and the alcohol helped us to relieve the tension that was building up before the event. When Pa's tension was released, he could go on with life. When Peter's tension was released, he could face the next battle.

I wasn't condoning the use of alcohol; I just was able to understand better why Pa and Peter used it.

I realized that all these events and thoughts were part of growing up. Responsibility was another aspect of life. One responsibility of mine was to prepare and maintain a garden if I was to eat this winter. Who knows, maybe Peter would be eating with me.

I looked around the yard. I could see how some flowers by the house or by the lane would improve the looks of my home, making others want to come to visit. Also a clean house would make a big impression. As I climbed the stairs after watching the sun set in its usual prairie glory, my head was full of plans.

Ellen's Story

By the end of May, the garden was dug, planted, and watered with water from the creek. Small flower shoots were showing by the house. Debris and garbage around the yard was taken care of. It looked quite nice.

Then I tackled the inside of the house, even to washing all the fancy dishes in the buffet. After all, war was over, people would be able to use their ration books to start the stove. People would be exchanging dinner meals again. Everything that was good and wonderful back in the 1920's would be good and wonderful again. So I even washed the fancy linens, hanging them out on the line in the breeze. They smelled so fresh after I had ironed them and put them back in their place.

I stored the diaries and Ma's Bible in a box in my room. The diaries were no longer needed. I knew where the Bible was if I became inclined to read it.

I cleaned my room and went to Ma and Pa's. It was empty except for a broom handle hanging horizontally from the ceiling holding only a few meagre pieces of clothing, including Ma's stole. I swept the wood floor, raising a great deal of dust. Then I washed it. Near the corner by the door I noticed a loose crooked board in the wall about two inches off the floor. I tried to straighten it. The small nail holding it in place came out causing the board to fall off the wall. As I made the move to replace it, I noticed three old tin cans in the hole.

Of course, I had to see what was in them. One by one, I took them out, and opening each one, I stared at the contents. Money. And lots of it, I think, for I didn't remove any to count it. All I could think of was it must be part of Pa's gambling money. I couldn't bring myself to touch it.

I replaced the lids, the cans, and the board. I finished washing the floor and shut the door. It was like shutting out another phase of Pa's life. I never went into that room again.

After doing all that dirty work, I bathed and washed my hair in the big washtub. Donning my nightgown and slippers and taking my brush in hand and the cup of tea I had made, I made my way to the bench.

It was near midnight. Many prairie nights are warm and free of the wind. This was one of those glorious nights. The stars grew brighter as a crescent moon rose in the east.

I brushed and brushed my hair, drying it as much as possible before plaiting it in one braid. Peter would surely call me his Lady Godiva now as I could just about sit on my hair. In the morning, I would take out the one braid, brush it again, and then make two braids that I wound around my head to keep it from getting in the way.

As I climbed the stairs to bed, I felt weary but content. I was clean, the house was spotless, and the yard was attractive. Peter should be home sometime soon now. July was not that far away. He'd be pleased with my work.

All that was left now was to wait for Peter.

CHAPTER 39

It was six years ago that Peter left for Europe. As long as war was raging, I had no waiting problem. I knew and accepted the fact that as long as there was war there would be no return of Peter unless he was severely injured. Now that the war had ended, the army had no more need of him so each day of waiting and watching was long and tedious.

Fall was approaching. The flowers had wilted with the first tinge of frost. The garden had been harvested and stored for future use. My meagre furnishings and bare wood floors had been kept in their spotless condition.

Mr. DeJong came for me with his wagon, this time pulled by the tractor—a sure sign of the returning prosperity.

Some foodstuffs were still rationed so I purchased what I could and received the back issues of the newspapers Mr. Black always kept for me. A short visit with them and then to the post office to find no mail waiting for me.

Conversation was at a minimal due to the loud noise of the tractor engine. After Mr. DeJong unloaded my coal, I offered him a cup of tea. He kindly refused, and I understood why; daylight was shortening, and he still had to reach home before dark being he had no headlights on the tractor.

Even understanding the situation, I was disappointed. My yearning for news of Peter's return was so great. No letter that day didn't help my personal situation either. The DeJongs seemed to change the subject when I would ask them if they heard any news. I was beginning to think that they had heard Peter would be returning in a poor condition, and they were so sad about it that they didn't want to talk about it.

That, too, I could understand. On many of my walking trips to town I would be there when the train came in. The platform was always full of expectant people, hoping that their loved one came home that day.

I would join the hopeful watchers but stood back so as to be inconspicuous. The DeJongs were never there which I thought strange, but the prospect of seeing Peter before them added excitement to the whole issue.

Tears of joy would fill my eyes when I would observe a fairly healthy looking soldier or airman hop from a still moving train to run for a woman running towards him. A heart-warming embrace, faces full of tears and kisses, a grab for his duffel bag, and they were gone amid a platform of cheers and good wishes and congratulations.

Other tears would cloud my vision when seeing an aging couple greet their son as he lay on a stretcher. Bravely they leaned over him to give him a gentle hug. He raised his arms to embrace his mother, one arm missing a hand and part of the forearm. His father shook the remaining hand and then guided his wife gently to the waiting ambulance that would take their son to the town's rapidly filling hospital. I wondered how bad his injuries were. Would he ever leave the hospital alive?

Various degrees of injured men and women disembarked the passenger train that had arrived behind a black steam-driven locomotive. Broken arms and legs, bandaged torsos and heads, some on crutches with one pant leg pinned up, some in good shape, others in a devastating shape as related above. But all had smiles on their faces.

I remembered when train loads of men passed through the station on their way to serve their country. How many of them came back? I will never know, and I guess it really doesn't matter except to their loved ones. They did their duty, and all of us across this great

country of Canada that Pa was so pleased about are grateful to them.
Bless them all.

Dianne Osborne

CHAPTER 40

Winter came, but Peter didn't. I made my trips to town when the weather permitted. Rarely, I went to DeJongs; Olga tired easily, especially now that she had two little ones to care for. I left them to their lives.

I started the second winter of being on my own with a little more fear and trepidation than last winter. My trips to town were quick as a blizzard could come up so fast here on the prairies. Getting lost in the blowing snow was not a strange happening. Newspapers usually had a few stories of snowstorm deaths. Who knew how many incidents didn't get printed.

I guess my biggest fear was that I would parish in a snowstorm before Peter arrived home. Believing he was just as anxious to see me as I was to see him, I thought how devastating it would be for him if he came home only to find me gone.

No matter how careful or conscientious one is, circumstances sometimes play havoc with our good intentions.

I started out one morning soon after daylight, which in midwinter is close to midmorning. The sky was clear, the sun bright, and the air crisp. Warm clothing and brisk walking would keep me comfortable.

I did my business in town and had a short visit with the Blacks. Still no letter from Peter. And no Peter hopping off the train that stood at the railway station.

The road out of town was a block away from the station. When the train was stopped, the length of it crossed the road prohibiting traffic. I checked the sky; only flimsy white clouds were visible. I will be able to watch the passengers who, by this time were mostly civilians with a few soldiers now and then, step down and move on

180

to their destinations. The train would leave as soon as all left the passenger cars.

Such was not the case on this particular day. The engine stood puffing more than a block away with no sign of a big puff of black smoke or a whistle to tell of its moving on. I waited and waited. Getting anxious, I went to the telegraph office to see what was the trouble.

"Hello, Miss Ellen," the kindly gentleman said as I approached his window. "What can I do for you?"

"I was wondering when the train was leaving. I can't go around it as the snow is too deep and fluffy."

"Sorry about the inconvenience, Miss Ellen," he said consternation in his voice. "I don't know when it will be leaving. The snowplow crew is cleaning the tracks of snow somewhere between here and the next stop. How long that will take I don't know."

Disappointment showed in my face. The day was going by seemingly fast. Going home in the dark was not pleasant but feasible. Going home in a sudden snowstorm was both unpleasant and unfeasible.

The telegraph operator tried to help me in a feeble way. "If it's too late I probably could let you sleep on the benches in here but it would be cold. I don't know…"

He was interrupted by the dot-dot-dash-dash of the telegraph machine. He turned his attention to it. In a moment he returned to me with a smile on his face. "I just got word they have cleared the track. The train should leave in the next few minutes."

"Oh, thank you very much," I breathed with relief in my voice. "Thanks, again," and I started walking to the road that led to home.

About a mile out of town, I noticed clouds on the western horizon. "Maybe they are slow clouds," I thought but hurried anyway.

181

Dianne Osborne

The wind picked up soon after that bringing the clouds across the sky in a flurry of snowflakes. By the time I reached DeJong's lane, the car tracks on the road were almost invisible as were the trees down the lane.

Stepping out from the protection of the lane trees, the wind hit me with all its fury. How far I could see ahead of me was hard to judge. All was white and, of course, my tracks made earlier today were gone. Even the road seemed gone with the blowing snow filling the ditches as it passed in front of and around me.

Another thing that was gone was the light in the window to guide me. There was no one at the house to light it.

Bravely, I moved on, not even thinking for a second to stop at DeJongs. They had sheltered me so many other times; they would have gladly done it again. Such was my concentration on getting home.

My one consolation was that there would be no coyotes out. They would be curled up somewhere beneath a bush of some kind sleeping out the storm.

As long as the wind continued to batter my left side, I knew I was still going in the right direction. Once, for only a moment, it abated somewhat. I luckily caught a glimpse of a grey shadowy structure I believed to be my house.

Suddenly, I felt as if I was climbing a steep hill. It was the pile of dirt that was the end of the road. I was at the east end of my lane.

Making a left turn into the wind, I stumbled, fell, and rolled down an embankment to thin crackling ice below.

I was in the creek. The creek ran close to the north side of the house.

"Follow the creek." The thought seemed to be coming from outside of me. Was it Pa? He always was wise in the knowledge of survival.

182

Ellen's Story

I followed that advice no matter where it came from. Another lull in the storm showed me the house. Scrambling up the bank, I passed the graves. "Thanks, Pa," I mentally said.

Reaching the back house, I used it. Stepping out into the wind again, I took hold of the rope that led to the wood shed then on to the porch. The rope was put there every fall and every winter. I was thankful it was there. Today was no exception.

I revived the fire in the stove and drank a cup of tea sitting on Pa's couch. The next thing I knew I was waking up to the warmth of sunshine through the living room windows but to the cold of a stove fire gone out.

I thought about my excursion. Providence, fate, God, whatever you want to call it, led me home safely. Although had there been more water in the creek I might have drowned.

CHAPTER 41

Ayear had passed since the war ended before I received word from Peter. It was just a short note saying: *"...much improved. The Canadian army is helping the British army to clean up many of the estates they used for hospitals and shelters for local and foreign refugees. I wanted to see the country under peace conditions as the people are so friendly and the scenery— the spots that are not blown up by bombs—is so serene. The lambs scamper here and there. It is so wonderful that children can do the same thing. Don't know when I'll arrive home. Depends on many things. Of course, I'll see Father first. It will be different without Mother. After that I'll pay you a visit. Take care. Love, Peter"*

It wasn't really good news but it explained many questions.

With a little lighter heart, I planted the garden and some flowers and kept the yard and house tidy and clean. The melting of the abundance of snow gave the creek a good flow of water from which I watered the plants.

By now most of the enlisted men from our town and area were back home, that is the ones who could return. A few memorial services were held at the various churches for those laid to rest in foreign soil.

Prosperity was also returning. Some local young people, as well as some newcomers, were searching for new homes, some in town and some in the country.

Many acres of government land lay north of the creek that ran past my house. Having to go miles out of their way to get on the other side of the creek deterred many would-be farmers. The municipality, with the prospect of good times ahead, took a chance and built a bridge across the creek.

The bridge was made of timbers and planks. Much dirt work was done by hand. When all was done, it looked sturdy enough for tractors and one-tonne grain trucks to pass over it. Big timbers standing on end, one on each side of the bridge and at both ends told the traveller where the edge was.

Towards the middle of September, the weather turned cold. An unusually early frost, rain, sleet, and even some snow played havoc with the grain crops. In a few days, it cleared, giving us a couple of weeks of Indian Summer. Beautiful warm days allowed the farmers to harvest their crops. When my 'harvesting' was done, I spent these lovely days outside, either soaking up the sun or walking the edge of the creek.

I decided to make one more trip to town on my own before the usual trip with Mr. DeJong to get coal and major winter supplies. Habitually, I went to the post office first, going up that side of Main Street, window-shopping as I went. Crossing the street at the post office and another session of window-shopping would bring me to Mr. Black's where I made my purchases and my visit with the Blacks and anyone else in the store.

On this day, as I was heading in that general direction and quite close to my destination, I noticed a young man with greying blond hair still in a somewhat military haircut coming out of Mr. Black's store. A petite, dark haired woman carrying a child, which I guessed would not be quite a year old, accompanied him. After he had deposited the groceries he was carrying into the backseat of a car, he helped her and the child into the front seat. At that moment, he happened to raise his eyes catching my person in his vision. A surprised look came over his face but quickly disappeared. He immediately got into his car and drove away, heading out of town on the road that passed my place.

"Must be one of the new people who have been moving in on the other side of the bridge," I thought. He looked somewhat familiar, but that didn't mean much. Everyone has his or her double.

"Or maybe he's someone I used to go to school with." I thought no more of it at the time.

Mr. Black's greeting, usually so warm, was not so on this day. It was not as warm although, as always, he was glad to see me. Yet I felt a subtle change. "Maybe his wife is not well," was my excuse for his cooler greeting.

"Oh, hello, Ellen," he said. Clearing his voice, he continued, "What can I do for you today?"

I told him my wants and needs, and as he was packing them into a brown paper shopping bag, I mentioned I saw many new faces in town. It was a common enough remark, one made by others since the new bridge was built. I added, "I just saw a couple come out of your store a few minutes ago. They headed out my way. Must be starting a new home on the other side of the bridge."

"Uh, yes, I guess. Yes, indeed, I guess so," stammered Mr. Black. "Well, there you go, Ellen, all ready for you," he said as he pushed the bag across the counter for me to pick up. "Have a nice day. I have some things to do in the back room."

It seemed to be a cold shoulder brush off such as the one the thrift store lady gave me a few years back. I didn't recognize it as such as I knew Mr. Black was a busy man and that he was one of my very best friends.

As I reached the door, he called to me in a very sincere and emphatic way, "God bless you, Ellen."

Touched by the tone of his voice, I sincerely and softly replied, "Thank you very much, Mr. Black." I left for home wondering why all of a sudden Mr. Black seemed to be so concerned for me.

It was still mid afternoon so I didn't need to hurry. It would be daylight until 6:30 or 7:00 p.m. As I walked, I had to change the shopping bag from one hand to the other, thinking that shopping was much easier with the sled.

Ellen's Story

On the way, I heard a vehicle coming behind me; the sound of the tires crunching on the gravel was heard above the putt-putt of the motor. Many times on my trips to town the neighbours would stop and ask me if I wanted a ride. Many times I told them that I'd rather walk as there was no need to hurry home. They soon stopped asking, but as they passed me, they slowed and waved to me sometimes shouting pleasantries. I would return the salutations.

Expecting to see a familiar face while preparing a friendly greeting, I was surprised to see a strange man slowing his small truck as he came along side of me. Protruding from beneath his peaked cap was a crop of bright carrot-red hair. His smiling round face sat atop broad husky shoulders.

"Hi, there," he called. "My name's Sean Healy. Can I give you a lift?"

His manner was pleasant enough, but I felt uneasy. Not wanting to be rude yet not too friendly, I calmly said, "No, thank you. I don't accept rides with strangers."

"Oh, I'm not a stranger. If we're heading in the same direction, we must be neighbours. Which side of the bridge do you live on?"

I continued to walk, looking straight ahead and saying nothing. I felt my Irish temper rising.

Hearing no answer from me, he tried other questions like "What's your name?"; "How long have you lived here?"; etc., etc. Still I did not answer.

Finally, he said, "Okay, I can take the hint. See ya later." And he drove off.

I proceeded on my way promptly putting Sean Healing or Healy or whatever his name was, out of my mind.

But the greying blond young man haunted my thoughts. He looked so familiar. Who was he?

187

The answer came a few days later. The weather was still pleasant, allowing me to spend my days outside. On this day, the blond man's car entered my yard.

I got up from the bench by the shed and came forward to see if I could be of some assistance. He slowly got out of the car and took a couple of steps forward. His face was sad, the tone of his voice when he spoke was cheerless but the words were beautiful. "Hello, Ellen. How's my Lady Godiva?"

Peter was the only one to call me 'Lady Godiva.' Was this somewhat muscular man sporting a greying moustache on his unsmiling lip tempting me into believing he was Peter?

Then I saw it. Even though his hair was quite short, that wayward lock was still determined to fall forward.

I froze. "Peter," I whispered. For seven long years I dreamed of this moment. In my dreams, we ran towards each other, arms extended. Peter grabbed me, swinging me around. We laughed, we cried, we kissed, revelling in each other's company. Now in reality, I couldn't move, only whisper once again, "Peter," while my hands lay crossed on my chest trying to still my thumping heart.

Peter stood silently a moment longer and then started to say the most horrible things.

"Ellen, this is very hard for me to say, but I can't marry you as we planned." He stopped to lick his drying lips and then continued in a rush. "I have never stopped loving you from the time we were kids. I flirted with the women overseas, but that was all until I could take it no longer. In Paris, I met Giselle who was lonely like myself. We went to a small hotel. Proprietors never asked questions. The war was on, making everything so different. Once I realized what I had done, I hoped against hope that there would be no consequences. But she conceived. The girl I loved couldn't conceive, the girl I didn't love, did. Ironic, isn't it?" He let a disgusted sort of chuckle

188

escape his throat. "Anyway, her father was adamant we should marry. So we did, waiting for the child to be born before we set sail for home. I've since come to the conclusion it was a set-up job. So many people are poor and destitute. If the parents could marry their daughters to foreign soldiers, it gave them some relief. I've also learned that I am not the only fool. But that's no excuse for hurting you."

He stopped talking for a moment. Was he waiting for a reply from me? A burst of rage? A flood of tears or curses? I was having a nightmare. In nightmares, you want to run away, but you can't. That was my condition at that moment. I remained silent so he lamely finished his sordid story of woe.

"I'll always love you. I wanted my homecoming to be so joyful and happy. I failed you, my family, and myself. I ask forgiveness but won't blame you if you can't do it." He hesitated. "I guess there's no more to tell."

Stepping back, he turned and opened his car door. Before getting in, he reiterated, "You'll always live in my heart. You'll always be my Lady Godiva."

He got behind the steering wheel, turned the car around, and drove out of my lane, down the road and into his father's lane. Although this news was devastating, I felt he was still part of my life.

CHAPTER 42

When I came to my senses, I let out my breath that I was subconsciously holding. My knees weakened. I sank to the ground and lay in a huddle on the dying autumn grass. Inside, I was dying. My brain and heart were not functioning; my body was cold. The setting sun brought the chill night air stirring life into my limbs. I went inside and sat on Pa's lumpy couch to stare at the night through the window.

So many things went through my mind, things that Olga, Peter, and I used to do together as if we were one family.

One of the things was the corncob pipes Pa made for us.

Ma would make soap out of the wood ashes, water from the rain barrel, and lye bought from the store. Mixing these ingredients in the right proportions would result in a pudding-like concoction that she poured into a shallow wooden box lined with a sugar or flour-sack cloth. When the soap was just about set she would take a sharp knife and cut it into 2" x 4" bars. When the bars completely hardened, Ma would wrap each one in a piece of brown paper saved from parcels bought at the store. They were then stored in a cool place.

For washing clothes, shavings would be cut from a bar and dropped into the water. In a saucer whose cup had been previously broken, a small chunk of a bar lay waiting for us to use on our own body while washing in a basin at the washstand.

On warm days, Ma or Pa would shave off small bits of soap to put in the bowls of the corncob pipes. Taking the basin that held some water in it out into the sunshine, we would dip the pipes into the water then blow on the stem. Rainbow bubbles of all sizes would float forth into the air. Sometimes we could get a big bubble coming out of the bowl of the pipe. By blowing carefully, we could get it as large as our heads. Then it would break splashing us with tiny droplets of water. We would laugh and try again.

I thought of those bubbles getting larger and larger, filling our hearts with joy and anticipation of great things. Then they would burst, coming to nothing.

I felt like one of those bubbles. For seven long years, my bubble grew with love, hope, and faith. In two minutes it burst.

Some inner voice kept saying, "All is not lost." Again and again, we built more soap bubbles. Again I'll build myself another bubble to fill again with love, hope, and faith.

"But what for?" I argued with myself. The answer was, "I don't know."

Alas, my bubble grew very slowly. At that time, love was the only thing I could blow it up with. I knew that I would never love another. Unless some unforeseen event occurred, I could see nothing in the future for me but spinsterhood.

I didn't cry for a long time. When I did, the tears were a mixture of joy and sadness. Although Peter was not with me daily, he was at least home; he was alive and only a mile away.

Mr. DeJong came to pick me up with the tractor and wagon to go for coal and winter supplies. I didn't go with him, as I knew it would be an uncomfortable companionship for both of us. He seemed to be relieved as I told him to bring me a fifty-pound sack of sugar and a hundred pound sack of flour.

About a week after Mr. DeJong brought the coal, Olga came to visit. I apologized to her for declining her offer of friendship. I told her I needed to be alone. She understood. It was many months before I saw her again.

I didn't go to town that winter. There was no need. My winter supplies from the garden and the store were already in storage. Because the war was over, there was no urgent need to know what was going on in the world, therefore no need to pick up any newspapers till spring. There would be no letters from Peter in the post office.

When my daily household chores were done, I would sit on Pa's couch and watch at the window. Now that the bridge was built there was more traffic. Sunday mornings, I would observe families on their way to church; a couple of hours later they returned home. Early Saturday afternoon brought families into town for their weekly supply of groceries. Some would not return until the beer parlour closed at 10 p.m.

One day, as I was cleaning my bedroom, I came across the doll Pa bought for me almost twenty years ago. She lay 'asleep' in the crude cradle Pa made. Her looks would make it easy to pretend she was real. I picked her up and cuddled her. My empty arms were glad of something to hold.

I took her and the cradle downstairs to Pa's couch. Many days, I would sit and hold her, rocking her back and forth in Ma's rocking chair while keeping my eyes on the window. The scenes varied from bright sunshine and traffic to swirls of whirling snowflakes that hid everything else from view.

On nice days, I bundled Kathleen up to take her to see her 'uncle' and 'grandparents' grave. Her head would bow or flop sideways but always glad to be there. The ever-present smile on her face told me she was a happy 'baby.'

Towards spring, I finally got a grip on myself. I was rocking Kathleen when my eyes were suddenly opened. I held her away from me and said, "Kathleen, I love you as a person tends to love things that bring precious memories back. You are only a doll but you gave me life. Now I can return you to your cradle and the corner in my room where you belong."

Ellen's Story

It took me over six months to come to terms with myself. Now I was ready to face life again. The first time I happen to see Peter will be the hardest, but it will get easier as the years go by. With just love in my bubble, it will grow very slowly.

CHAPTER 43

Out of habit as well as necessity, I planted a garden in the spring. The flowerbeds were cared for, not with the excited anticipation that I felt the year before, but with a bit of contentment. This is my life now. I may as well get used to it.

I started going to town again. Whenever Peter and I saw each other, we would look into each other's eyes and then continue on our way. Giselle was quite attractive with her short dark hair and eyes. The child, a boy, had Peter's blond hair but his mother's eyes– quite striking and handsome. Each time I saw them, my feelings were a mixture of agony and happiness. I ached for Peter's arms around me, but I was glad I had the chance to look upon his face.

I came down with a summer cold or so I thought. I felt dragged out. I blamed a persistent cough for that. It became a real chore to hoe the garden or to wash clothes. I was accepting more rides from the neighbours on my trips to town.

On one such trip, the traffic was sparse. I was almost to town when I became dizzy. I tried to get to the ditch to sit on the grass till it passed. I don't know if I made it or not. Blackness set in.

I was aware of strong gentle arms lifting me and setting me in the front seat of a vehicle. Then the doctor was at the door asking me questions that I was having difficulty to answer for lack of breath. A cough that brought up a little bit of blood cleared my air passages letting me talk. The doctor didn't seem to be listening. He was ordering the driver to take me to the city TB sanatorium.

The staff at the sanatorium was waiting for me as the doctor had telephoned ahead. Sean was tested as a precaution and then released. I was tested and x-rayed to determine the extent and category of my disease–the one that took the lives of Pa, Ma, and Mrs. DeJong.

Ellen's Story

Results showed my condition to be not severe but more intense than in the case of Olga. It would be three years before I could once again look upon Peter's face. This time my memories would give me visions of a young man, a man I could be proud of.

My new home was in a fair-sized room that I had to share with three other ladies. Curtains, which ran on rails attached to the ceiling, could be drawn around each bed affording privacy to the individual. Each of our cocoons housed a bed, a bedside table and a comfortable chair. A row of lockers stood by the entrance door to accommodate our belongings. A small bathroom with running water and a flush toilet took up one corner of the larger room.

A closed curtain around a bed signalled the desire of the individual to not be disturbed. I was too ill to want to associate with strangers even if they were in the same predicament as me. The girls respected my wish for solitude–I slept most of the time–retiring to the common room to read, piece together jigsaw puzzles, or just quietly chat.

As medication and rest started working their wonders on me, I slowly made my way into the circle of TB patients finding support and encouragement. I was happy to return the favour as new patients filtered in.

Autumn turned to winter bringing Christmas. A week before the big day, I received mail. There was no return address, but I knew the handwriting as if it were my own. I opened the envelope with shaking fingers. It was a beautiful Christmas card bought especially from a drugstore shelf. "To Someone Special" was embedded in the glitter of Christmas bells and holly. Inside was a professional loving verse. It was signed simply, "Love, Peter."

I clutched the card to my breast. Silent tears of joy ran down my cheeks. He still loved me. Was it right for us to love each other when he had a wife? I didn't know the answer. I only knew wife or no wife, there would be no other for me but Peter. I was willing to become a spinster if need be.

As the winter winds blew, I grew stronger in body and mind. I contemplated my present situation. I was ill but I was living like a queen–electric lights, telephones, flush toilets, central heating, food bought and prepared for me, no dishes to do, and no floors to scrub.

I reflected on my past. So different it was–filling the kerosene lamps and cleaning the glass chimneys every day. When there was no kerosene, candles had to suffice. Such dim light yet at the time so welcome.

Communication was talking to someone face to face after having walked to his or her home. Hauling in coal, chopping wood, and emptying ashes, all dirty chores that made the house dusty, provided heat. Bathing was carrying water from the well or melting snow and then throwing the dirty water out one pail at a time. Using the facility meant dressing in scarves and wool coats if it was winter. Summer wasn't so bad. Groceries were hauled home on the sled. The cooking range had to be fired up winter or summer for making meals. In summer it made the already warm house hot. Wood floors were scrubbed on hands and knees with a brush.

I looked to the future. All I could see was two years and a little more of living in luxury even if it was a sanatorium. After that my mind went blank.

My bed was by the window. Many time, I would look down on the street three floors below. It was always busy, always cars, delivery trucks, bicycles, and people.

I never realized how much people meant to me. The few people I really knew were precious to me. Circumstances didn't allow them to be ever present in my life, and I learned to live without them. During my convalescence, I looked forward each day to say, "Good morning," to my roommates. After a day of fellowship, we crawled into our beds with 'sweet dreams' echoing in our ears. When I needed my privacy, all was needed was the pulling of my curtains and it was granted.

During my private times, my thoughts invariably turned to Peter, but they were always of Peter and me in the past. On Pa's old couch, I used to plan the future. Sitting on my comfortable chair in my cocoon, a blank was drawn. Yet in my heart Peter lived. Always there was that tiny ray of hope.

That ray of hope broadened one day in the very early spring of 1949. Snow was still on the ground, but spring was on the way. Back home, Olga would wear out the pages of the seed catalogues while attending to her new little seedlings. The men of that household would be attending to the newborn calves and foals and planning their fieldwork. Yet there was still time for relaxation before things really got hectic.

Whether or not Peter had time to write letters, he did write one to me. It was not a pleasant one.

"*...not realizing the danger she was in. All winter Giselle had talked of petting the new "baby cows and bulls". We told her that would be fine but be careful. I don't know the details: Tom, Father, and I were in the barn; Giselle was in the pen, unknown to us, with the cows and their calves. While revelling in the joy of the calves' saucy faces and petting the soft fur she didn't notice a calf's mother until it let out a bellow which brought us out of the barn in time to see Giselle fly over the fence to land on her back motionless on the ground. The doctor said she was already dead when she hit the ground. The cow flipping her with its horns had broken her neck. It was...*"

My letter-laden hands dropped to my lap, my eyes stared at my privacy curtain but didn't see it. A little later I finished reading the letter, it was just a few trivial sentences simply signed *"Peter"*.

CHAPTER 44

How do you react to news like that? While it opens up the way for more dreams of Peter and I together, there had been no other correspondence between us to let me see or surmise the depth of his love for his son's mother. "Out of sight, out of mind," so the old saying goes. Peter had not seen me for about a year. Yet he hadn't seen me for seven years coming back with a wife and still declaring his love for me.

I was stunned. I was numbed. In a few days, I wrote a small sympathy note to Peter including the rest of the family in my condolences. That was about all I could do. I had to let time take its course.

A couple of months later, I received a letter from Olga. She was quite irate. Reading it made me realize she wrote like she talked–just one thing after another.

"My dear Ellen," she wrote. *"What a terrible winter we have put in. The snow was piled high at times. Little Thomas just couldn't get to school. Poor fellow. He's just in the first grade. We have to take him to the same school we went to but he doesn't have the joy of friends or older siblings to walk with him. We had so much fun, going to and coming from school, didn't we, dear Ellen. I feel sorry for little Thomas as well as the other children attending that school. There's been talk of closing the school and taking the students into town with one of those big yellow school buses you see in magazines. Can you imagine how horrible that would be? The driver would probably make you sit still and be quiet. I can't see that would be much fun."*

She went on about this and that and finally came to what I believe was the real reason for writing to me.

"...buried in our family plot. A few people came after the service in the Catholic Church—she being French was, of course, Catholic—as most people didn't know her. They came I think for Peter's sake.

Ellen's Story

One person that came was quite obnoxious and presumptuous. He's only lived on our road on the other side of the new bridge—I still call it new even though it has been there for almost four years—for only a couple of years. I think you know him a little; at least he was the man who found you on the side of the road. That's the rumour anyway. His name is Sean Healing or Healy or something like that. Well, anyway, I was not pleased with what he said to Peter and Peter knows I'm not pleased. I probably shouldn't be telling you this but I just have to, dear Ellen, because I've always considered you as my sister even if Peter married another woman. I just feel you should know what this man said to Peter.

He came to Peter and shook hands with him saying "Sorry about your loss. In a way its kind of like my loss too."

Peter frowned and asked, "What do you mean?"

"I've been asking around about Miss Ellen Woods. They tell me you were pretty sweet on her at one time."

"What are you getting at?" Peter angrily asked.

"Well, without the first Mrs. DeJong around, you and I just might be competitors."

I thought, dear Ellen, that Peter was going to hit him. Instead he got real close to the man's face and snarled, "You go to hell, fat boy."

With a smirk on his face this Mr. Healing or Healy or who ever he is, turned and walked away.

I was so disgusted with that overweight pig. I'm sorry, dear Ellen. He makes me so mad I could spit.

I was and am happy to know that Peter still loves you. And I still love you. Maybe I shouldn't have told you the bad part but I did so want you to know the good part.

Oh, my goodness. My potatoes are boiling over. Got to go. I'll write again. Try to write to me.

Love you as a sister, Olga."

Dianne Osborne

Well. Well. Well. I never. I was so mad I could have spit, too. I ran for a piece of paper and pen. I have to write to Olga was my first thought. But when I sat down to write, nothing would come to mind. What Olga told me was bad news. No, it was good news. Oh, I didn't know what kind of news it was. I was upset. "Calm down, Ellen. Think about it for a few days then you'll be able to answer sensibly."

This I did. On the roof top of the sanatorium was a closed in garden. Plants grew in pots, small ones and big ones, that protected the patients from the sun. Chairs and tables and benches mingled among the plants to make a paradise complete with birds and sometimes butterflies. Here it was that I sat often pondering the situation. Each solution seemed to come to a dead end.

Until one day.

I immediately wrote to Olga. I thanked her for letting me know what happened; I let her know I was as angry with her and I, too, loved her as a sister. *"But I need to ask a favour of you. Sometime when the men are away from your house for quite some time, take yourself up the road to my house. Wear a cloth over your nose and mouth, as it will be filthy in there. Go into Ma and Pa's room. Behind the door in the corner, the bottom board is loose. Remove the board and the three tin cans that you'll find there. Do NOT open them. Later I'll tell you the contents but for now please do not open them. Hide them some place in your house and DON'T say a word to ANYONE. I know it is still a little more than a year before I come home but I BEG you to keep the lids on the cans and on your curiosity. When you have done this, write to tell me you have done it. I will then let you know the rest of my plan. Love, Ellen."*

CHAPTER 45

It wasn't too long before I received a letter from Olga saying that she did what I bid her to do. As I guessed, she was full of curiosity but promised to say not a word. I felt I could trust her. My fulfillment of the bargain was not to come for a few days yet. First, I had to write to the reeve of the municipality whose office was in our town.

I wrote:

Dear Sir:

Due to the condition of my health I am unable to speak to you personally. The condition of my health is the reason I am issuing the following request.

Since being in the sanatorium I have learned a great deal about health issues and sanitation. I have come to the conclusion that the buildings I own— house, barn sheds, etc.—on the property near the recently built bridge north of town should no longer be used. They are contaminated and should be burned. Nothing should be saved.

I have money to pay for the labour, etc. needed to do the job but am unable to obtain it until I am released from the sanatorium. Please trust me, I will pay immediately I return.

This letter gives you permission to destroy my buildings in the name of health.

Yours truly,

Ellen Woods

P.S. Please inform me when it is done and also let the DeJongs know what is intended as they are more or less caretakers of my property.

Miss E. Woods

After sending the letter, I felt light headed, I felt mean, I felt cruel, I felt kind, and I felt joy. I wanted to run and dance and sing and I wanted to sit still and gloat.

201

For almost two years, I lived in a state of a type of luxury with hours and hours of time on my hands to do as I pleased. I was thrilled at the chance to read the books in the institute's library, feeding my thirst for knowledge. The daily newspaper kept me well versed in current events and upcoming trends in living and technology—a real big, new word for me.

I was thankful I could pull my curtains around me and ponder quietly what was happening in the world but most important what was happening to me. As a child, I was rich. I had Ma and Pa, the DeJongs and Pa's dreams. The slowness in the turn of events mesmerized me into a state of oblivion. Sitting in my cocoon, my eyes were opened. As soon as my release is cleared, I will spring forth like a butterfly. Using Pa's money, I will buy new clothes; I will build a new house with all new conveniences; I will buy a car to go to work rather than depend on someone else's handouts. I will tell Mr. Fat Boy to go chase himself.

Even with all these beautiful dreams, I knew I would let them go if and when Peter asked me to marry him.

I received Olga's letter before the councilor's letter. It began *"Dearest Ellen. How could you do such a thing. All your belongings. All your books and keepsakes."* And on and on and on. Olga couldn't understand and yet she should have. Maybe her sojourn in the sanatorium was closer to her own home life that she didn't notice the difference. But then again, Olga was not a thinker. An idea was there and immediately acted upon. And I loved her for it.

Olga said she cried as she watched the brilliant flames reduce Pa's dreams to ashes. Yes, Ma's Bible and diaries were gone, Kathleen was gone, and Ma's rocking chair and Pa's couch, all gone. They had served their purpose. It was time to move on.

"Peter was so strong and solemn as he quietly watched, not saying a word. When everything was just a pile of burning embers I saw him heading down

along the bank of the ravine towards our cave we three used to play in. I couldn't understand why he would go for a walk down there."

But I could. Without realizing it, Olga told me the greatest news anyone could give me. Peter was also yearning for me.

The last eight months of my stay at the sanatorium seemed to drag, and yet all of a sudden my release was only a few weeks away. The letters between Olga and I fairly flew, each telling of the excitement of coming home, what it would mean to each of us.

"For the first week you will stay with us. Father is adamant about that. He's quite pleased and proud of you for what you did to your place. I'm beginning to understand a little. But never mind that. Our first week will be spent shopping for clothes for you. Won't that be fun. Then we'll have a homecoming party for you. I've found some lovely hors d'oeuvre recipes…" Her plans went on.

I, on the other hand, had other plans, vague, but still there. I would let Olga have her way for the first week.

The day of my release I said good-by to my cocoon. As I looked at the bed, the table, and the chair, I realized that this very minute corner of the world had given me life in more ways than one.

I went down to the receptionist to sign myself out. Peter had written many times, each time declaring he and his father would be there to take me home. After all, they were the only family I had. Even with all the ups and downs and hurt feelings of the past, the DeJongs were still my family.

I descended the stairs with trepidation. This would be the first time I would see Peter so close. He had always signed his letters *"Love, Peter"* so I knew our greeting would be joyful. There would be no hugs, too many people around for that. I was sure that would come later.

203

Dianne Osborne

My heart thumped radically but stopped in horror as I stepped into the reception foyer. Large as life and looking very smug about it was Mr. Fat Boy–Sean Healy.

He came forward extending his hand–which I refused–saying "Hello, Ellen. I've come to take you home. Peter couldn't make it so he asked me to come."

Disbelief and shock showed on my face to the extent a staff member asked me if I was all right.

I said, "I need to sit down."

She guided me to a chair and went for a glass of water. All this time Mr. Healy stood over me gloating.

The nurse came back with the water and my release papers to sign.

"Sign these papers, and then you'll be free to go with your friend," she said pleasantly.

"He's not my friend," I shouted. Tears came to my eyes. "He's just a big fat man who pushes his way around. I'll die here before I go home with him."

The tears fell. What went wrong? Where were Peter and his father?

I heard the nurse ask him, "Are you not Mr. DeJong?"

He said, "No. I'm Sean Healy, another friend of Miss Woods. Mr. DeJong was unexpectedly unable to come so he asked me to pick up Miss Woods."

I jumped to my feet shouting, "That's a lie. He hates you as much as I do."

"You're so right, Ellen" a wonderful familiar voice said as a man came through the door. Peter walked up to Mr. Healy and advised him, "You had better leave peacefully and right now or I will call the authorities to charge you with harassment."

Ellen's Story

The fat boy's face turned white, then red. Not another word came from his mouth as he quickly left.

Peter turned to the nurse explaining, "I've had some troubles with him so I checked him out. He has a habit of harassing young women. I would advise you to warn your staff about him."

Turning to me, Peter asked, "Would you like to sign your release papers and come home with me?"

I didn't have to be asked twice. A quick good-by and many sincere thank yous and I was out the door on the arm of the only man in my life.

CHAPTER 46

It was a beautiful August day, not only weatherise, but also I was on my way home.

Where home was going to be, I wasn't sure, but I knew it would be so much better than before.

As we entered the yard, Olga and Tom waited on the steps. Olga ran to me as I got out of the car and hugged me with all her strength. I felt at that moment we were truly sisters; we had gone through so much of the same traumas. She had to release her hold on me to dry her joyful tears and blow her nose on her lavender scented handkerchief.

I turned to Tom and hugged him, too. He whispered in my ear, "Do you think you could forgive me?" I whispered back, "I already have." He, too, wiped his eyes. It was only he and I that would ever know the reason for his tears on that day.

Even though I had just spent the last couple of hours with Mr. DeJong, I went to him to shake his hand. "Thank you for so much, Mr. DeJong. There were many times I was not the nicest of persons yet you continued to help me. For that I'll be forever grateful."

Now it was my turn to ask for forgiveness, and he whole-heartedly gave it saying, "Of course, I forgive you Ellen. You didn't have the best of lives. Your Pa was…well, we'll talk of that another time. Today is a day of rejoicing and gladness. Come, Olga, bring on the food I know you've been working diligently at preparing."

Peter stepped in then and said, "I have a little something I'd like to show Ellen first. If you'll excuse us, we'll go look at one of the flower beds Ellen used to help Mother with."

We went to the other side of the house out of their sight. We stood and admired the roses and other plants still growing there after all these years. Then Peter said, "We've been through some hard times, Ellen. No doubt we'll go through some more, but it would please me immensely if you would go through my hard times beside me as my wife." He produced a tiny box holding in it a sparkling diamond ring.

Ring or no ring, I whispered "Oh, yes, Peter. Yes, yes."

He slipped the ring on my finger. Tenderly and gently, as was his nature, he took me in his arms kissing me with a warmth and passion I felt right down to my little toe. What joy! What ecstasy to be in Peter's arms and to know I would be there for as long as we both lived was extra special bliss.

When we came back and the announcement was made, there were more hugs and kisses. Little Thomas and Eva—how they had grown—and even Peter's son, Stephen, got into the act. Olga brought out the food as we were to eat out on the picnic table by the spruce trees where Olga and I had shared our cookies with the birds so long ago. Mr. DeJong went to his shop and brought back a bottle of his moonshine.

We sat on lawn chairs, later settling our repast. Olga suddenly jumped up, broke a lull of contentment, and demanded, "Ellen, whatever is in those cans?"

"Cans?" the men chorused. I laughed. "Go, Olga, and bring them here. I will satisfy your curiosity."

I sat on the grass in the midst of my family—so good to think of them as my family—and slowly removed the lids. Their eyes grew as big as saucers; their mouths gaped. "Money," they all breathed at once.

I told them where it came from, how and when I had found it, and what I had decided to do about it. "When you wrote to me, Olga, about Mr. Healy, I was afraid he might go prowling about my place and find these cans. Needless to say, I spent some anxious days until I came up with my idea. I know everything there was my past, but as I learned more and more about sanitation, I knew I would be sick the rest of my life if I went back to that house and that way of life. Everything had to go. With this money, Peter and I can build a pleasant house with conveniences that will make our lives, as well as the lives of our children, so much more pleasant. On the day of our wedding the land will also belong to Peter to farm to the best of his ability, and I will support him with as much strength and ability as I can."

Peter came to sit beside me putting his arm around my shoulder and his lips on my cheek. It was as if no one else was there as he gently kissed me on the lips.

Suddenly, Mr. DeJong's declaring broke the quiet, "Time for another drink. Ellen, where's your glass?"

I replied, "No, thanks, Mr. DeJong. I have had enough. I've learned to know when to quit." Through laughter, we reminisced about the day we learned the war was over.

Night fell on some very sleepy but very, very happy people. We said our goodnights, but when I said, "Goodnight, Mr. DeJong," I received a reprimand.

"Young lady, that's enough of that; to you the name is Dad."

I agreed as he gave me a fatherly hug.

Peter escorted me to the guest room and opened the door. "It will be wonderful when we can enter the same room together. Until then, I'll just say, 'I love you'."

Ellen's Story

EPILOGUE

Peter and I had been separated for twelve years. I was sixteen when he left for Europe. I was twenty-eight when he carried me over the threshold of our new home built on Pa's land and with Pa's money.

We lived comfortably with our son—our little French lad with an inherited wayward lock of hair—and our blue-eyed, red-blond daughter. We prospered, working the land diligently, having sensible goals to guide us.

Guiding us also was faith, hope and love, qualities we intend to pass on to our children.

Tradition is something else to hang on to as well. Each night as Peter and I prepare for bed, Peter finger-combs my hair over my bare breasts and reminds me, "You'll always be my Lady Godiva."

Printed in the United States
138475LV00001B/6/P